CW01640647

THE SPIRIT

OF

THE FEN

Terry Reeve

Terry Reeve © Copyright 2008

All characters are fictional and any resemblance to persons
alive or dead is entirely coincidental

All rights reserved

No parts of this publication may be reproduced, stored in a retrieval system, or transmitted in any form or by any means, electronic, mechanical, photocopying, recording or otherwise without the prior permission of the copyright owner.

British Library Cataloguing In Publication Data
A Record of this Publication is available
from the British Library

ISBN 978-1-84685-949-6

First Published 2008 by
Exposure Publishing,
an imprint of
Diggory Press Ltd
Three Rivers, Minions, Liskeard, Cornwall, PL14 5LE, UK
WWW.DIGGORYPRESS.COM

FOREWORD

This is a novel for Bungay, about Bungay, written to extol its assets and its beauty, particularly Outney Common, fictionalised here as Bungay Fen. It is of course fiction - all the characters and bodies of people involved in the story are made up, and any similarity to people or groups living in the town, or any companies depicted, are co-incidental, though the story is set in Bungay and the physical aspects of it are as they are in reality. The story does not judge the stance of anyone or any group living in the town today.

It is a story which is particularly topical, however. With the Government wanting more and more homes built around the country to meet the demand, more and more will have to be built on greenfield sites, particularly in rural counties such as Suffolk. Planning guidelines are being loosened all the time. This story may be set in Bungay, but towns and villages up and down England will be able to identify with it, the characters portrayed and the concern and heartache and aggression that can come to the fore when green areas are threatened.

It is a story of our modern time.

Terry Reeve

This novel is dedicated to the community of Bungay

IRIS GLADE

Down and through the Iris Glade
From the sunshine into shade,
Through the birch and bramble curtain
To a haven sure and certain;
Into green and peaceful ways,
Into gentle twilight haze,
By the rippling river where
You are at one with God, and share
With Him a silence full of words,
And see the shadowy night-time birds
As low across the marsh they glide
In search of food for nests that hide
Within the covered Vineyard Hills.
This is a place where all your ills
Are soothed and healed by nature's balms,
And by an atmosphere that calms.
A world that surely God has made
When you go through the Iris Glade.

CHAPTER ONE

DANNY hurried through the old market town, across the footbridge over the bypass, and down on to the Fen. Dusk was beginning to fall, and it was cool at last – or at least cooler than it had been that hot, humid July day, particularly in the classroom, where the children had been restless and fretful. It had been a job to get them to concentrate on anything.

The school day done, it had been three hours of catching up with paperwork and reports – he was already behind, and the head was pressing for completion by the weekend.

Then a snatched meal, and a history society committee meeting, thankfully not too long, partly due to two of the older and usually most loquacious members dozing off. Danny had taken his leave as soon as he could, gone home and donned shorts and T-shirt over his tanned body, put eager collie Megan on her lead, and made for the peaceful sanctuary of the Fen, 400 acres of grazing meadow and heathland, broken by copses of silver birch and scrub oaks, gorse, hawthorn and extensive wild blackberries.

Now he took off his old trainers and half closed his eyes in the bliss of hot soles on the refreshing grass – cool, caressing, draining away the stresses of the day, and soothed further by the myriad pot pourri scents of gorse, and dyke and slight evening mist.

This fenland was his sanctuary, his retreat, his special place, which had drawn him ever since he was a boy, and swam and fished in the river which surrounded it on three sides, encircling it in a great, protective loop.

He made for the furthest point of the river now, down the track trodden out over centuries of use, to a screen of silver birch trees, where the path made its way between blackberry bushes and ferny undergrowth. There was no breeze, just the occasional noise of Megan moving through the ferns on her never ending trail of investigating the source of those powerful but elusive smells that only dogs enjoy. She would be ahead and then behind, her sheepdog instinct ever there, worrying that Danny was where he should be, but finding plenty of time to roam, nevertheless.

Through that screen was another world, especially now on the verge of dusk. Beyond it was an open area of meadow, the grass high with summer, but barely moving, just the slightest of evening whispers breaking the silence now and then. Over to the left were copses of trees, and a rustic fence and dyke to the right, splashed with the yellow of flag irises in the spring, marking where the grazing meadows began. Iris Glade it was often referred to by local people, because of the tall yellow flowers that adorned the dyke in late spring in unusually large numbers. Cows grazed now, placidly, silently, statue-still, soon to become silhouettes in the fading light.

About 200 yards ahead was the river, at its furthest point of its huge meandering loop around the Fen on the north side of the old town of Bungay, and beyond that, and beyond more meadows of the flood plain, criss-crossed by drainage dykes and fences, rose the Vineyard Hills, the Suffolk borders' concession to high ground. Thickly wooded with oaks, birch and beech – and once many elms – they rose steeply to meet the sky, dark against the deepening blue as the stars began to come out to pinprick the heavens as delicate sparkling jewels, setting off the centre-piece of the creation, the crescent moon now rising steadily behind Danny's right shoulder as he walked steadily towards the river, and his favourite spot of all, the narrow railed bridge, crossing the dyke which ran at right-angles into the river there.

The scent of the gently flowing Waveney – centuries ago it was thought to have been called the romantic sounding Avona – fused and enriched by the countless aromas it picked up as it touched its changing banks of grasses, wild flowers, sand, reeds, cultivated fields nests and fallen trees along its 25-mile course to that point – was so strong now, so intoxicating, relaxing, stimulating the senses, as Danny came to the bridge and lent on the railings, with his back to the hills and the river, facing back to the town, now in dark, angular outline through the trees on the other side of the Fen. He could just glimpse, through a gap, the tower of St Mary's Church, standing in the centre of the town, symbolic of it, and of constancy and security in an ever-changing world.

Megan sat down beside him, resignedly – she knew they could be there like that for some time. It was what her master did on the Fen walks, part of his re-newing routine. But faithfully too. She knew that where he went, she would be too.

And what did he think, that master of hers, as he stood there, taking in that scene, heavy with symbols, a spiritual haven with its audible, evocative silence?

Danny thought many things, recalled many memories, and dreamed many dreams there, in his favourite spot in the whole of the universe, as he watched nature at work.

There if you were lucky, you could see the flash of electric blue and orange as shy, darting kingfishers, heralded by their piercing cry, momentarily skimmed the river surface and disappeared as suddenly as they had come. And you could stand for some time there, and watch barn owls on their sorties from the Vineyard Hills in search of food for their young, systematically combing the area, and suddenly dipping down out of sight, to emerge moments later with a vole in their claws.

Stand perfectly still, as Danny and Megan often did, and they would pass within 10 yards, unaware of the human presence, as they headed back to their oaken nest.

You would see cuckoos, too, in the spring, not just hear them – often two at a time as they went about their parasitic job of finding a nest in which to deposit their eggs. A linnet could be the unsuspecting victim – there were many of them among the gorse bushes, more common even than the skylarks which soared above the Fen in the summer sun, and nested in the deep heathery grass. The cuckoos would sit calling at the top of birch or oak or willow trees, and then fly off to another part of the Fen.

And in the river, a sudden splash could be a large pike feeding, or an otter playing or diving for fish from its riverbank retreat.

Danny looked around him, from the Vineyard Hills, across the grazing meadows – for centuries known as The Lows – and scanning then the higher heath ground, known as The Hards, and back to where he stood on the bridge. In that 400 acres, at a conservative estimate, there were around 250 species of flora, and an unknown number of fauna, all nurtured there by nature over centuries, untroubled.

What fascinated him as he stood there was that, apart from fencing along the dykes, and the glimpsed church tower, you could see nothing man-made – everything in that landscape was completely natural, as it had been since time began. The Fen was an area of land largely left to itself, and the marshes on which the cattle grazed had had that use for probably 1000 years. Neolithic man had worked beside those meadows, on the ground, 5000 years ago, when the sea had still penetrated there and what was now known as the Fen was the start of a wide sea estuary.

The only buildings there had ever been on that land would have been the primitive and transitory structures of pre-historic man and, much more recently, a pest house which was there for about 40 years in the 18th century, and grandstands when horse racing was in its heyday in the first half of the 20th century. They had long since gone – the only buildings now on the Fen were the golf club house, and the water pumping station, in its own enclosure in the centre of the high ground, and well screened by trees.

Just one other building was prominent in this largely unchanging scene and one which to Danny was idyllic, beautiful and very much part of his childhood and youth. That was Vineyard House.

Vineyard House nestled at the foot of the Vineyard Hills, on the opposite side of the river, facing towards Bungay. Thatched and pink-washed, with diamond-paned windows and lawned gardens stretching down to the water's edge, it was a picture of peace and serenity in the hazy distance as you walked from the town, and Danny coveted it, as did many others who knew it.

"When I make my fortune, I shall buy that house," Danny had told various lovers he had walked with on the Fen over the years. "I'll make the owners an offer they can't refuse. It is such a beautiful cottage in such a beautiful place."

As he looked at it now, over his left shoulder, the lights shone from its windows as the dusk deepened, making an even cosier, yet more alluring picture, one dating back nearly 400 years, when the hills would not have been wooded, but when the vineyards, planted in the early years after the Norman conquest by the barons who were quickly allotted lands and settlements as reward for their allegiance to King William, had long since been cleared.

Danny sighed. "One day," he thought. One day…"

What was it about the Fen that moved him so, stimulated his mind and clarified his thinking? It was all these things. And it was the silence too – an almost tangible silence in the stillness of early night. Expectant, almost. Yes. It was almost as if it was waiting for something momentous to happen. Some formidable challenge to everything about it that people held so dear in their hearts and minds.

"On summer evenings, when the shadows are long and the grass is high, when the cattle are statues in the grazing meadows, and the sun still warm and drawing out the fragrances from marsh and gorse, when swifts and swallows chase playfully beneath the blue sky and the river drifts, sultry slow, through the peacefulness: this is my favourite Fen time, when the stillness is undisturbed, and you can dream your dreams and walk closely with God."

Danny had written that once about the Fen, as a testament to how it inspired him.

"You could not be there, at times like that, and not feel spiritually lifted by the scene. It can only convince you that this was all created by some higher being – that God is there, and is working in this place," Danny thought now. "I feel so close to God here. I know He is here with me. It is such a strong and powerful feeling. How do the words of the hymn go? 'Be still for the presence of the Lord, is moving in this place.'"

And if the Fen and its atmosphere moved him, how had it moved much greater people who had known it, and had been there?

William Butler Yeats poem about Innesfree seemed to tally with Danny's feelings for the Fen, too.

"I will arise and go now, and go to Innisfree,
And a small cabin build there, of clay and wattles made.
Nine bean rows will I have there, a hive for the honey bee,
And live alone in the bee-loud glade.

"And I shall have some peace there, for peace comes dropping slow,
Dropping from the veils of the morning to where the cricket sings;
There midnight's all a glimmer, and noon a purple glow,
And evening full of the linnet's wings.

I will arise and go now, for always night and day
I hear lake water lapping with low sounds by the shore;
While I stand on the roadway, or on the pavements grey,
I hear it in the deep heart's core."

Yeats clearly sought a sanctuary too, thought Danny. And he thought of the Fen's fascinating history, turbulent sometimes, as it had evolved from true common land to come to be owned by a group of people known as the Fen Wardens. Exactly how that had happened was lost in history, and written evidence was scarce, but over 250-300 years, by usage, they had been deemed to be the rightful owners. It was something which many local people resented, and more recently it had been challenged at an inquiry before a Government inspector.

People had claimed the Fen should be registered as a common, as common land, the realm of the community, but after a lengthy and sometimes acrimonious hearing, the inspectors decided that the Wardens had exercised ownership over it for so many years, in selling parts of it, and accepting rents for it and payment for materials gleaned from it, that he could not declare it common land.

It meant that the Fen Wardens, who managed it and drew dividends from it, were the rightful owners. And after the decision, their chairman had declared that Bungay people would continue to enjoy the privileges they had enjoyed over the land for centuries, provided they respected the use of the tenant farmers who grazed it, and the golf club which rented the course and fairways.

But its beauty, its openness and its atmosphere had captured the hearts and imagination of many people over the centuries.

It had inspired the great painter Sir Alfred Munnings, who first got his love of painting horses when a friend took him to a race meeting there around 1900 – on the day, in fact, that he heard he had had his first works accepted by the Royal Academy.

It had inspired Sir Henry Rider Haggard, that writer of classic adventure stories. It was the view from his study window as he gazed out towards the town from his home on the north of the river, not far from Vineyard House, seeking creative inspiration for his works such as King Solomon's Mines, and She.

And then there was Compte Francois de Chateaubriand. His was a fascinating story, part of Bungay's history and, Danny always thought, Bungay's greatest love story, involving the man yet to become great, and Charlotte, the teenage daughter of a Bungay clergyman, the Rev John Ives. After he fled the French Revolution, he injured himself while horse-riding in Beccles, and came to Bungay to convalesce at their home in Bridge Street. He fell in love with Charlotte, and Danny was convinced that during their frequent convalescent walks on the Fen they came to love it as a beautiful sanctuary, to appreciate its birds and flowers and trees, in the same way that he did.

Chateaubriand was one of France's greatest statesmen, perhaps the greatest of the 19th century, and one of her greatest authors. Yet his autobiography, a classic of its kind, dwelt at some length on his relationship with Charlotte, his dramatic departure from Bungay after Mrs Ives offered him Charlotte's hand in marriage (unknown to the Ives, Chateaubriand was already married), his coming to fame in France as one of its greatest writers and a leading European statesman, his return to England some 20 years later as ambassador to the court of King George IV, and his emotional meeting with Charlotte, by then Lady Sutton, and their wistful last parting when she returned to Bungay. They were to never meet again, but their deep love for each other was clear. Danny knew the story almost by heart.

As he stood on the bridge in the deepening twilight he recalled the loves he had courted on the Fen - most recently Jenny Rogers, though she was not a lover, more a close friend whose mind tallied with his in many respects and they enjoyed often deep conversations as they walked arm in arm there.

Jenny was a reporter with The Waveney Gazette, the local daily paper, and they would often confide newsworthy information to each other. Jenny loved the Fen in the same way that he did, and they had come to relish their walks there more and more.

The last time, two or three weeks ago, on a day as hot as the one just ending, they had swum in the river at midday and then lain on the grassy bank of the Waveney in the sun, and enjoyed the scents of the grass close to their faces, of the riverside reeds and the grazing pasture and their drying bodies.

"Isn't is beautiful, this mixed aroma of scents. They come directly from nature," Danny had observed, as he lay with eyes half-closed.

"Mmm, absolutely heavenly, but you only catch them as strongly as this once in a while," Jenny had murmured.

"Like now you mean? Well, my Gran had a theory about that, and I think she was probably right. She used to tell us that when you are a child you can smell the flowers strongly, because you're small and your face is closer to them, to the scents and fragrances. But you don't consciously appreciate them – that only comes when you are older, and the scent of flowers and shrubs remind you of times gone by, and places you knew, and friends."

Danny paused to swat a horse fly, and then continued:

" Only then, you don't catch those fragrances and memories so often, because you are grown up and your face is further from them. When you do the scents are as beautiful, if not more so, than the memories, but you have to consciously reach for them to catch them. And sometimes, hard as you try, they seem elusively out of reach, and your hand stretched out for those rekindled fragrant memories clutches only the breeze, and leaves you empty."

"But we are enjoying them at the moment because we are lying down beside them, sharing their closeness. Mmm, seems logical."

"Yep. On this Fen the scents of the gorse are so strong, so powerful – so heady. When the sun is on the gorse the scent is almost tangible, isn't it…it is almost like a potion, an elixir. You almost feel that a few lungfuls of it could cure you of anything. You could make a fortune if you bottled it!"

"It is a lovely theory. Your Gran was clearly a profound lady."

"No, not really. I think she just enjoyed nature, and appreciated it in all its guises. She was a woman of the countryside."

Danny thought about his Gran, his mother's mother, now as he stood on the bridge. She was a woman of great inner strength, firm beliefs, a confirmed Christian and regular church-goer. But she had a great sense of humour too, a mischievousness almost, and as a child Danny has always enjoyed the times he spent with her.

He would go with her to Holy Trinity Church for Sunday services. He understood little of the liturgy at that age, but the words of the hymns and the prayers remained somewhere in the recesses of his mind, and for some reason the name Pontius Pilate in particular. He kept it with him wherever he went, often mouthing it under his breath, as a sort of comfort companion.

He told Jenny about it on another occasion they were lazing in the sun on the river bank after a cooling dip.

"I had a friend called Pontius Pilate once, you know!"

"Pontius Pilate! Sounds like a pompous pilot to me! Do you mean the Pontius Pilate who was Jesus' friend?"

"Hardly a friend!" Danny protested mildly, turning over so he lay on his back and could look at the sky against the top of the chestnut trees on the other side of the river. "He betrayed Jesus as surely at Judas did. He had no guts, no principles, no…He just wanted to please as many people as he could, and he did. He knew Jesus was innocent, but he betrayed Him."

"He didn't betray Him, whatever he did." It was Jenny protesting, conversationally, now. "He was just weak, dominated by his wife. He just washed his hands of Him, that's all. He didn't condemn Him."

"No he didn't – he let the rabble do that. He was weak – afraid of them, so he made no decision himself. He hid, and that is worse, it was as bad as condemning Him. He betrayed him, whichever way you look at it."

Jenny was still lying on her stomach, her eyes closed, enjoying the sun. "It can't have been easy for him," she said. "He had that mob baying for Jesus blood. They'd have lynched him if he had declared Jesus innocent. It would have taken supreme courage, and he was an ordinary man, after all. Why are you so hard on him? Do you find decisions easy always?"

Danny was silent for a few moments, his eyes watching occasional clouds, moving almost imperceptibly, high in the sky.

"No, no I don't I suppose. Maybe that is why he became my imaginary friend – we are like minds. I know there have been times when I have known what was right, but have shied away from doing it, or saying it, just to keep the peace. Why does there have to be animosity, and aggression, and confrontation?"

"Maybe because without it there would be anarchy?" said Jenny rhetorically. "Come on – this is getting too serious. How did Pompous Pilot become your friend, anyway?"

"Well, I was introduced to him at Sunday School, I suppose – friendly chap, basically, all dressed in white, with a white face, sunken eyes, bushy eyebrows, thong sandals."

"He took Sunday School classes did he? I always suspected you were mad, but now I know it!"

Danny turned and smacked her shapely bottom in its diminutive bikini.

"No he did not, or I'd have told him what I thought of him." He paused, and then went on:

"As far as the New Testament is concerned there are three key people that always stand out in my mind…well four, of course, including Jesus. But the others are Peter, Judas… and Pontius Pilate, and for some reason I latched on to him. He was just one of those imaginary friends, a comfort friend, I suppose. My brother went everywhere with a Father Christmas toy when he was small; my sister had an old cot blanket she would never be parted from. My comfort took on an imaginary guise – Pontius Pilate.

"I guess it was just that every week at Sunday School, or at church, we all said the Creed, by rote. You know…'suffered under Pontius Pilate, was crucified, died and was buried. On the third day He rose again from the dead, and entered into heaven, and sitteth at the right hand of God, the Father Almighty, from whence He shall come to judge the quick and the dead…' Something like that."

"…'I believe in the Holy Ghost, the Holy Catholic Church, the communion of saints, the forgiveness of sins, the resurrection of the body, and the life everlasting. Amen,'" Jenny continued.

"Very good!" Danny mocked. "No. I think my subconscious liked the structure of that name, Pontius Pilate, that's all, and as a child I kept repeating it. Mum said I was always talking to Pontius Pilate when I thought I was alone. I adopted him as my friend, and I can remember talking to him myself so it must have gone on till I was five or six, I suppose. I found it easier to talk to him than real people, maybe – I didn't have to commit myself. I washed my hands of things in the same way the real Pontius Pilate did. He was an imaginary friend but I took on his personality in reality."

He had rolled over and was looking into Jenny's eyes. An earnest, almost haunted, look had come over his face.

"It's uncanny. Now I'm stuck with it forever – I know what I should do, what I should say, sometimes, but I take the easy way instead."

He almost spat out the words. It startled Jenny. She stared back at him for a few moments.

Then she stretched out her arms, put them round Danny's neck, pulled him down on her, and held him tight.

"Come on Daniel! That's enough deep talk for one day, specially a day like this. Let's get back in the water. Its so inviting. It makes me feel sooo sssexy!"

CHAPTER TWO

BACK home in his terraced cottage in Quaves Lane, Danny opened all the windows to let the evening air in, took his T-shirt off, got a cold drink from the fridge and went and sat outside on the rustic bench on his patio, picking up the latest edition of the Waveney Gazette from the table as he went. Megan lay down nearby. The sky was dark now but the spot was lit by the light from the kitchen window.

The air was still warm, still drawing out the scents from the late flowering orange blossom, and the rambling rose which covered a trellis and wooden archway which separated the patio from the small garden beyond. It faced south west, and was a suntrap by day, with a view over towards the Fen, though the fenland itself was not visible from the garden, the view being interrupted by the gate towers of the ruined Bigod Castle around which the original medieval Bungay was built. The castle stood on high ground, at the neck of the huge loop of the Waveney which cradled the Fen within the borders of its silver ribbon – a fine defensive position, protected as it was on three sides by the river and marshes from which, in the days it was built, it would have been virtually impossible to mount an attack on Bungay. The town's medieval street pattern was made around the castle and Bungay's two churches, the Saxon towered Holy Trinity, and the larger more dominant St Mary's in the centre of the town.

The Fen and the town complemented each other. Bungay was not well blessed with recreational areas but the fenland made up for that – it was its huge communal back garden and playground, where informal football and cricket were played, where generations of townspeople learned to swim in the river, go boating, walk, gather blackberries, or walk the dog, or where the children would create their own adventure games and, later on, do their courting among the gorse bushes and the soft ferny grass that carpeted the Hards.

Danny stretched, settled into his seat, took a long draught of drink, and picked up the Gazette.

At first, the front page headline did not register fully in his mind:

FEN HOMES PLAN REVEALED.

It was only when he read the opening paragraph of the lead story, at first idly, that he focussed fully on it:

"AN ambitious £400 million scheme which would see Bungay's ancient Fen transformed with luxury homes and wide-ranging community and river-based facilities was announced by developers yesterday.

"In what would be by far the biggest development the town has ever seen, Cambridge property developers Pilgrim Homes Plc have submitted a plan which would see 2000 houses, a new community centre with function hall, a sports centre with football, cricket, tennis and bowls facilities, established there.

"A boating clubhouse with bar, children's adventure playground and skateboard park, a restaurant and pub are other aspects of a scheme which would see the town's population almost double."

Danny sat up, his mind suddenly sharply in focus. Surely this could not be a serious possibility? The rest of the story dispelled that hope:

"Company boss George Bell said the plans had been finalised following lengthy negotiations over several months with representative of the Bungay Fen Wardens, who hold the freehold of the 400-acre common, and it had now been made public with their blessing.

"Their chairman, Fenton Skipper, said the overall scheme would provide the town with the sort of facilities it could only otherwise dream of, and would more than make up for the loss of some of the common land – much of it would still remain available to the public through the impressive facilities in the Pilgrim plan.

"The news, revealed exclusively today by the Gazette, has also received a cautious welcome from town council chairman Adam Neil-Davids.

"'There are clearly many aspects of this to consider and the council will be holding a special meeting in due course to discuss it fully. But it provides exciting possibilities for Bungay, its people, its many voluntary organisations, and of course commercially,'" he said.

Danny read on, disbelievingly, about a scheme which had been given the name Iris Glade by the developers – a name locals had given to that picturesque parts of the common where the copse of silver birch and oak trees led through to a clearing, towards the river which seemed to have a spirituality all of its own, a special peace between the trees and river which seemed somehow sheltered from the outside world. A place which was Danny's retreat from the day.

He read that the company was hoping that if planning permission was forthcoming work could start within a year on the first homes, and that even for a company which had large developments throughout the east of England, this was one of its most imaginative and ambitious schemes for which it hoped to have the support of the local community.

In return, the story said, Bungay would get facilities that would not attract public finance to enable them to be built, and were unlikely to get National Lottery or sports development funding – there was a diminishing "pot" now available following a seemingly limitless supply over the past few years. It was a golden opportunity to make Bungay the envy of any other town of its size.

"What rot! Bungay is the envy of many towns because of what it is! What utter nonsense!" Danny breathed angrily to himself.

The special town council meeting would be held at the Fisher Theatre to enable as many people as possible to hear the discussion, and would take place before the district council met to make its decision on a plan which one planning officer said was unique in his experience, and raised many interesting points, though it was too early to say what recommendation they would be making to members of the planning committee.

Danny stood up, and threw the paper down, startling Megan, who also sprang to her feet and barked.

"They can't do this! They simply can not do this!" he said out loud. "Surely this cannot go through? They cannot do this to our common. It is already the finest amenity of any town of its size."

He sat down again, and tried to gather his thoughts in a logical way. The Fen represented 400 acres of largely untouched land, rented by farmers for grazing, and by the golf club for its 18-hole golf course. It contained rare plants and grasses, was a haven for small animals and birds. It was an environmentally sensitive area as far as planning speak was concerned, and officially designated as an area of outstanding natural beauty. Organisations like the Suffolk Wildlife Trust would be outraged at the very suggestion that it should be built on. There would have to be an exceptional reason for developing it, and Bungay did not need new homes – hundreds of ugly, chimney-less boxes had been built in the past few years on the other side of the town, he told himself.

No – this must be pie in the sky, a plan put forward by a big company to give its design department some creative work experience during a quiet period, and not one it realistically expected to win permission for. It was just an exercise – the plan would probably be withdrawn even before it got to a council meeting, and if it did the town council would voice strong opposition to it, and the district council would surely give it simply formal consideration before refusing it.

Subconsciously there was a picture of the Fen in his mind, and that and the mental exercise calmed him a bit. He picked up the Gazette again, and tried to scan through the rest of the Bungay news – a preview of the annual Bungay Festival and its range of cultural, recreational and sporting activities, the continuing town centre traffic problems, a nun from the local convent who had just got her karate black belt, one of the town's leading businesses, Devereux's Brewery, facing financial difficulties and shedding staff, final preparations for the town's Bungay in Bloom entry, another serious crash on the Halesworth Straight…

But Danny found it hard to concentrate. The story about the Fen would not leave the forefront of his mind. Phrases from the front page nagged away at him, and he finally turned back to it and re-read it, and looked at the pictures illustrating it – a typical panoramic view of the Fen, with the Vineyard House in the distance, and a picture of Fenton Skipper leaning on one of the gates, with a copy of the plans in his hands.

Danny had always found Fenton – more usually called Fen or Fenny - a friendly man, positive, conciliatory and good humoured. He would say himself that he had the right name to be chairman of the Fen Wardens - the Lows, where the cattle grazed were a fen after all, and as chairman he was skipper of them. And he would laugh his shy and genuine laugh, his head with its thinning hair slightly to one side, whenever he made the remark, and would endear people to him. Thinking of it now gave Danny more re-assurance – under Fenny's leadership the Fen Wardens would not sell Bungay down the river. He saw the Fen as part of Bungay's rightful heritage, and though it may be in private ownership, he often spoke of the people's right to walk there freely and enjoy their recreation.

The next day was Saturday, and Danny rang Jenny Rogers first thing in the morning. They had not met for a couple of weeks because she had been on an assignment away from the area, but he was sure she would know more about the story and be able to set his anxious mind at rest. She had been on the staff for several years, was a senior reporter, well respected in the town and someone who knew what was going on. She would know some of the background surrounding the application.

"Hi, Jenny – its Danny."

"Oh, hello Danny – I thought I might get a call from you before long!" she replied cheerfully.

"About the story about plans to desecrate the Fen with housing and all sorts of other things you mean? It will certainly worry a lot of people, but it won't go ahead will it? Surely it is just a paper exercise."

"My feelings precisely when I first heard about it. There are various designations protecting the common from this sort of thing: area of outstanding naturally beauty, environmentally sensitive area, valuable recreational area, wildlife habitat and so on. It shouldn't stand a chance. And it floods easily."

"But…?" Danny sensed Jenny was about to qualify that, and pictured her rather doleful but pretty face under its dark, short-cropped hair with is natural hint of curliness, taking on a more serious expression. He was right.

"But, yes, Pilgrims see it as a serious proposition. I've spoken to them and they have done a lot of homework on getting the scheme together, and spoken to a lot of people. I don't know much about the company yet, but it has a reputation of having a ruthless streak, and for getting permission for projects which on the face of it should be thrown out by the planning authority without a second thought. And from what I can gather they have big money behind them. I don't know if you ever heard about that scheme at Cherry Gunton, one of the most picturesque villages in Cambridgeshire? It is a lovely development, homes well built and to a high standard, attractively laid out and with lots of facilities the village did not have before. That was built on what was once partly common land, in the original sense of the description, belonging to the community and not privately owned. There was a quite a battle but, it got permission. That must be six or seven years ago, and now people have forgotten all the controversy and are enjoying the other benefits it has brought."

Danny winced inwardly as he listened.

"Jenny, what are you saying – you sound as if you are supporting this Iris Glade scheme. You sound as if you are saying it might get permission. Am I hearing this from you? I and many other people would never accept that happening to the Fen. I'm not concerned that Cherry Gunton people let them get away with it – they won't get away with it in Bungay."

His voice rose as he finished the sentence, and Jenny sensed his anger.

"Danny, Danny - you and I have enjoyed many walks on the Fen – our Fen, Bungay's Fen. You know I'm as horrified as you are at the thought that it could be lost to development, and if there is to be a concerted campaign of opposition launched against it I will give that as much space in the Gazette as I can. You and I know what that piece of land means to us and many other people. I don't have to spell that out. But there are those who see it as just that – another piece of land, so let's develop it and make a fortune from it. They will put up some very cogent arguments in favour of the plan, they will get knowledgeable people to support it, experts in planning law to argue for it. And believe me they have friends in high places, and friends in the right places, and if they haven't got them they have ways of winning them over to their point of view. This is a £400 million scheme.

"I don't want it to happen any more than you. I enjoy the Fen as a haven and a sanctuary just as much as you do The Gazette could take a stance on it, even launch a campaign against it if the editor thinks that is right. But Pilgrims are serious about it, have no doubt about that. They will have done a lot of work behind the scenes and will be doing even more between now and when it comes before the district planning committee. It is not a foregone conclusion that they will turn it down."

Now it was Jenny's turn to imagine Danny's expression, of pain and horror. He would be running his free hand through his brown hair, beginning to fleck with grey now from its 43 years of eventful life and his usually good-humoured face would have a drooping frown. She knew how much he loved the Fen and its special, spiritual atmosphere, and his daily walks with border collie Megan – a place to escape from the day to a realm untouched by changing times. She knew also that in his heart of hearts Danny knew the scheme was a serious threat to the very nature of Bungay and its rich character and history they knew and loved. His silence was short.

"What about the Fen Wardens, Jenny? Are they really in favour of it? I cannot imagine Fenny would have anything to do with this, and they all get a pretty healthy dividend from their goings – would they want to lose that?"

"Compared to their share of what Pilgrims would pay for the land the dividend is less than peanuts – you can work that out, Danny. And Fenny? Well, he is one of the few exceptions among the majority who see their goings purely as an investment. They have no concerns about the history or the aesthetics or Bungay's feelings for the Fen, its just a business for them and this is a pretty good business proposition. Fenny would have spoken strongly against the plan to them, and advised them against it, but he is only the chairman after all, and once the wardens have made their majority view known, he has to voice that publically as if it is his own view also."

They talked for a while longer. Jenny made it clear that the Gazette would be regularly featuring over the coming weeks a story which was the biggest to hit Bungay for years. It would follow it closely, blow by blow, every twist, every controversial comment, every picture opportunity. But it would not predict the outcome of the planning application.

Later Danny called on Fenton Skipper. He invited him in and they sat with coffee in the sun at the back of his house where the immaculate garden stretched down to the river, and hens and geese clucked and honked in another area of his land.

As he had suspected and Jenny had predicted, he sounded almost apologetic that the wardens had had discussions with Pilgrims, and not only that, had reached agreement by a large majority to welcome the Iris Glade scheme.

"Look Danny, you know me. I don't want this plan any more than you do, and I voted against it because I look at it as you do – part of Bungay heritage, a timeless land, a place where people can roam at will and enjoy nature and all its seasons. But that is just my view. There are over 80 common owners now, many of them don't live in Bungay and have little interest in it. They simply bought a going or two as investment and want to see the best return for it, and you can imagine the sort of pressure Pilgrims would put on them."

"So they'd sell their soul for a few hundred pounds?"

Fenny put his cup down and looked at Danny, hesitating. Then he said:

"We're not talking about a few hundred pounds here Danny. This a huge scheme and the stakes are high. Look, I shouldn't be revealing this, but I know it won't go any further than you. Pilgrims are guaranteeing each and every fen warden a dividend of £75,000 if the scheme gets planning permission..."

Danny's expression and rapid exhaling of breath said everything about his re-action.

"Yes...and at present the annual dividend is around about £100 per going. Not many people could turn that sort of carrot down, especially when you remember that a lot of the wardens are small farmers struggling to make ends meet in the present farming climate. Can you blame them for supporting it? Pilgrims mean business, Danny, and it is huge business – make no mistake about that. They will put a very strong case to the planners, and have persuasive lawyers to argue it if it goes to appeal."

Danny was struggling to take this in.

"You mean you think they will get planning permission?"

"I don't know. But if they don't it won't be for the sake of trying, and they will try everything. At that level of business, there are few scruples, believe me."

"But you will argue against it?"

Fenton lowered his eyes and studied his coffee cup carefully.

"Danny, I'm chairman of the Fen Wardens. I advised against it at the meeting. But I'm fortunate, I've had a good business, I've retired, and I'm more than comfortably off – I don't exactly need £75,000. But most of the wardens do. And now they have decided in principle, at a properly organised meeting, to support the application and sell the freehold of the Fen if permission is given, that is the view I have to voice on their behalf, as chairman and therefore their spokesman. My personal view matters not, now. I'm sorry."

Fenton was a man of honour and integrity – qualities that do not always act in favour of those who hold them. Danny could readily understand how hard it was for him to be the spokesman for views he did not personally hold, but he was not the sort to resign his position because of that.

His heart sank, and he put his head in his hands. He now studied his coffee cup as it began to dawn on him that this planning application that would see the ancient Fen disappear for ever was not just a paper exercise – there was a serious possibility that it could happen, and he was finding it hard to gather the many thoughts running through his head.

"I'm not saying it will go ahead..." Fenton tried to give him a semblance of re-assurance, "...but I don't want to pull the wool over your eyes. If Bungay is to mount a fight against the plan it needs to know it will be a very tough battle, and probably a costly one."

Danny knew, deep down, that he was right. Not many Fen Wardens had Bungay's traditional interests at heart, and those who did were elderly on the whole – indeed some who might have opposed it vigorously had died in recent years. And he understood Fenton's position, as chairman.

"I understand all this Fenny. I've spoken to Jenny Rogers of the Gazette, and she holds a similar view. But, well…this has come as a bit of a shock – there will be many people in Bungay devastated to hear this news. I'm surprised it hasn't got out before now though. These things usually have a habit of leaking out before they get to such an advanced stage."

They were standing now, and Fenny gave him a sympathetic pat on the shoulder.

"I'd have told you if I could, you know that. I'm a Bungay man, I've enjoyed the Fen over the years, same as you have. I don't want to see this happen any more than you, but we'll see. It may not happen."

CHAPTER THREE

DANNY returned home, had a bite to eat, put Megan on her lead and made for the Fen. It was still hot, with the sun burning down. It had been largely dry for some weeks, and the Hards, the higher ground where the golf course was and where cattle were no longer pastured, were looking arid and yellow, but The Lows retained their greenness, and the cattle were enjoying the pasture, but not the flies that persistently covered their faces as they chewed the cud, sat languidly on the grass, or drank from the dykes. Were they ruminating? Danny did not know, but he ruminated himself as he walked, mulling over in his mind what he had read, and his conversations with Jenny and Fenton.

In some ways, news of the scheme for the Fen should not have come as such a surprise. For some years, articles in national newspapers, and television programmes, had focussed on the need for more land for housing to accommodate the growing demand. Figures of many thousands for single counties alone had been bandied about. How they were estimated he did not know - no doubt some statistician had come up with them. And Danny had sensed that the mood of the Government was to relax guidelines in building on green land, rather than tighten them as is came under ever-increasing threat.

Of course there were also articles and protests over the issue - he remembered particularly one leading actor who had returned to his roots in rural Wales, a beautiful haven of rolling green hills, streams and waterfalls, full of wildlife and full of peace and contentment. He had found a wide tract of it developed with housing and sliced through by a motorway, and the headline on the article he had penned for the newspaper evocatively conveyed his heartbreak and dismay:

"What have they done to my Valley?" it read plaintively.

That was a few years ago. Much more recently, much more locally, the question of finding land for housing when brownfield sites - those previously developed in towns and cities but now derelict - proved inadequate had become a talking point and was frequently highlighted at debates in council chambers when planning applications were on the agenda.

Less than two months ago, Danny now recalled, he had been startled to read in the Gazette:

"Some of the most beautiful parts of the Waveney district around Beccles and Bungay and the Blyth Valley around Halesworth could lose their special protection from new development.

"The southern side of the Waveney Valley, the Hundred River Valley and the Blyth Valley are all designated special landscape areas because of the beauty of their scenery.

"But new Government guidelines say such designations should be scrapped as they may unduly restrict development. Now the district council is asking people for their views on whether to retain the special landscape status..."

Danny had responded to that with a letter which left the council in no doubt that his view was that the special status designation should remain and if possible be strengthened. He had felt that the panoramic views of the beautiful rural scenery of the Fen and other areas of the Waveney Valley, not to mention classic landscape areas in the rest of the country, should be protected.

But he had not believed that the relaxing of the guidelines in any event would bring applications to build within those landscapes themselves - certainly not on the Fen, even though, just before the second world war, there had been an application to build factories on part of it. The outbreak of war had put an end to that.

And Fenny was right, too, about the small farmers, many of whom were among the Fen Wardens. Farming had taken a lot of set-backs in recent years, as European

Union regulations squeezed their profits with greater restrictions, and two outbreaks of foot-and-mouth disease, not to mention the CJD virus which had ruined many cattle farmers, had together seen many go out of business - in some tragic cases it had led to suicides. Farming had become an altogether different business to what it was 30 years ago, and in the more extreme cases profits had diminished almost to nothing for what was a 24-hours a day, seven-days-week commitment.

It was no wonder that those farmers who were Fen Wardens had jumped at the chance of the big money on offer for the sale of the land for development.

Now there was this scheme to build houses and other facilities on the whole of it - this land where Danny now walked among the gorse and the blackberry bushes, the grasses and flowers, the birds and the small animals, through clumps of trees and beside dykes and the river, beneath a wide sky. It was something difficult to come to terms with.

"What will they do to our Fen?" he said to Megan.

The Bungay Choral Society concert filled Holy Trinity Church with sound. The main work that night was the first part of Handel's Messiah, and the 60 voices performed it well - controlled and full of expression, capturing the feeling and meaning of that great classic, Biblical work, celebrating the birth of Christ. The second half of the concert featured medieval Christmas songs and madrigals, relaxing and beautiful.

As Danny sat there taking in the music and the scene, the Christmas candles and flowers, the Nativity scene in front of the chancel, the Christmas tree somehow bringing out the warmth of the tableaux of the stained glass windows, and the eyes of the singers sparkling in the light and their concentration, he watched the faces and the expressive joy that was in them.

It called to mind something his grandmother had once told him many years ago:

"The minds and hearts of those singers are full of the words they are singing - they believe all the goodness and peacefulness of those words during the time it takes to sing them, you know, and they completely become those things. But only for a while, only as long as it takes to sing them. Then other thoughts take over."

And she was right in her way, though she didn't say it very well, thought Danny, as he watched the faces. The singers were feeling the music, believing the words they were singing - words of faith, compassion, love, sacrifice, jubilation and exultation. They were completely wrapped up in them, their minds empty of everything else. And yes, if they could contain that state of mind, that perfect goodness, not righteousness, beyond the end of the song, beyond the end of the concert, beyond the end of the day, into their daily lives, they could achieve so much with it.

If only you could bottle that pure belief and spiritual strength that can last such a fleeting moment, a harmony of pure music and Christian words and thoughts, you could change the world, he thought. But it lasts such a fleeting moment in time.

Only the individual himself, or herself, has it in their gift to recognise it, grasp it, and use it. And it would take such inner strength to do that.

He talked to Jenny about it when they next walked on the Fen. It was late afternoon, and the twilight was early and frost cold. Everywhere was already clad in winter's white mantle moulded closely to the trees and gorse and the sleeping grasses, and the curtain of Iris Glade, and their breath, and Megan's, vaporised on the still air.

"Yes, I think I understand what you mean," said Jenny, a slight note of doubt in her mind.

"Most of the time, somewhere inside them, most people want to do everything right by God - even those who say they are not Christians. Deep down they want to be, say, unselfish, put others first all the time, be understanding, help others when they have important things to do themselves, give to those worse off than themselves, have sort of...well, sort of clear consciences all the time."

"Yes, sort of. It's just that when they are singing the words that are of complete faith, untainted by any outside influences, anything secular, that purity of mind shines in their eyes and on their faces, whatever age they are - they are living the words, and it is as if they would love to live them all the time. But in this world so many things get in the way and it is impossible to do that."

"Unless you are a nun living in a nunnery I suppose," Jenny suggested, cuddly close to Danny for warmth as they reached the silent river at the bottom of the Fen.

"I guess so. But what can nuns do to influence the outside world, convert it to their pure faith? They can contain purity of mind and deed within the walls of their convents, but how can that affect the outside world? Surely the example they set is too self-contained, when to be of real worth it has to be spread far and wide. And anyway, there has to be the challenge of bad things in the world to battle against - fatal viruses, illness, war, whatever - the powerful negative things to stimulate positive people to action. That sounds odd, doesn't it, but do you know what I mean?"

"Yes, I do. But, well, if you want to get deep, darling Danny, it is all tied up with emotions, isn't it. Situations drive emotions - if you are singing beautiful words to beautiful music you feel you are part of, while you are singing, and for a while afterwards. But if you are fighting someone and the emotion is anger then that is to the fore during the fight, and for a while afterwards. And so on."

"Right, but with some people anger is the dominant emotion, with others it is gentleness, others compassion, others hatred, others have a dominant killing instinct maybe..."

They stood on the bridge now, facing towards the town in the distance as they always did when they reached that point, and Megan sat down, resignedly.

Would this be a long wait, or a short one, the expression on her face seemed to ask.

"You see," Danny continued, "this feeling I had as I sat and listened to the choir is part of a deeper theory I have. I don't know if I can explain it very well, but: I just think that every soul, new born - maybe even before a child is born, has every conceivable emotion available to it in equal measure - love, hate, sacrifice, graspingness, envy, lust, compassion of course, the ability to murder, the ability to lay down their own life for someone else, melancholy, cheerfulness, forgiveness, vindictiveness - you know, the whole range. That is before anything in this world can have its influence on which ones become dominant in a person.

"So why does someone became a murderer or warmonger and another work for good and harmony and would not hurt a fly? It's not just to do with the sort of family they are born into or the sort of people they come to mix with, or their genes - you hear of the nicest, best adjusted family in which someone is immensely cruel, or worse; or the most cynical, calculating family in which one will emerge who is compassionate and has complete faith in what is good. Why should that be? What governs which emotion becomes dominant in a person from the whole range that is with them in embryo? It is something indefinable."

"Wow, you're beginning to lose me now!" said Jenny, the length of her vaporised breath before her indicating the exhaled surprise in her voice.

"I have an idea what you're getting at, but you can't get away from the fact that it is outside influences, social influences, family influences, other traits in their own character, that shapes what people become."

"But there is the theory that they start with the whole range at their disposal. They start with a purity of soul - they must do. The Vicar said at a christening the other day, in his address, that the baby was not old enough to have sinned. They become tainted by living you mean.

But with some it becomes purer by living despite all those influences."

"Danny, you are a gentle man, reasonably modest - very loveable. But this business of the plan to destroy the Fen has brought your anger and resentment very much to the fore, inwardly and outwardly."

Jenny looked him straight in the eye, caringly and inquiringly.

"If something is deep in your soul, as the Fen is in yours, it can stir any emotion, good or bad, to the surface, and you can't control that. Come, on, let's get back home."

CHAPTER FOUR

ROBIN ANDERSON was late getting away from his business meeting in Bury St Edmunds. It should have finished at 5.30pm, but dragged on a further hour, and by the time he was in his car he had just 40 minutes to get the 50 miles back to Lowestoft for a much more crucial district council meeting.

The very future of Bungay Fen, known as Outney from Saxon times, could well depend on his being there, to cast his vote at the end of a debate on the most far reaching planning decision the council had ever made, certainly in his 20 years as a councillor for Lothingland. Every one of the 48 votes to be cast on the application for a massive housing and recreational transformation of the ancient Fen, once offering grazing rights to every inhabitant of Bungay, was likely to be vital to the outcome.

There had been intensive lobbying from all sides - the Save our Fen campaign mounted within 24 hours of the plan being made public six months previously, the Bungay Fen Wardens, keen to rake in a massive dividend from their goings on the common, the affordable housing lobby, and the new community centre project - the developers had promised to provide a much needed new purpose built £2 million community centre, complete with after school club and adventure playground facilities as part of the development if it went ahead.

And then there was the developers' own systematic campaign to persuade the community and councillors of the many advantages the development would bring to Bungay and the wider area; trying to influence the environmentalists with promises of riverside havens and wildlife areas; the common owners with blatant offers of inflated dividends; and the council with areas of affordable housing, and a housing scheme in general which would make big inroads into the target figure for new housing the council had to meet in the next 10 years. Not to mention the community centre carrot.

As it became clear that the key district council vote was finely balanced, the developers' strategy became more and more aggressive, even to the extent of veiled threats to council members. One Bungay councillor had spoken out to the Gazette, claiming she had been told her corner shop general store, in the town centre, would be put out of business if she did not support the Iris Glade project - that shops provided on the development would include a large store which she could have the franchise for in return for her vote.

Jane Fulcher had worked hard to build up her business from scratch and wanted to keep it where it was, in the town centre with easy access for all her customers. She had no interest in relocating to the edge of the town. But Pilgrim Homes boss George Bell categorically denied any threat or intimidation of her - they had simply been canvassing the views of all commercial and trades people on the viability of a scheme they saw as saving Bungay from steady economic decline.

It was just one of the stories the Gazette had carried over the past four months as it kept the issue in the forefront of public interest - background features on the history of the Common, the way it already served the town as a huge recreational asset which could never be replicated artificially, and the famous people whose lives had been touched by it - painter Alfred Munnings, classic adventure author Sir Henry Rider Haggard, and the great French and European statesman Chateaubriand.

There had also been stories, which no one would be quoted on, of more serious intimidation of councillors by Pilgrim Homes directors and their agents - even to the extent of threats against lives, the paper claimed. It quoted some councillors anonymously, one saying he felt uncomfortable about going out, and felt the council should have nothing to do with applicants who resorts to such tactics. Once again the company's agents condemned the reports as scurrilous and without foundation, and said they would not hesitate to take legal action if those claiming such things were identified - they were cowards to hide behind anonymity, and the newspaper was an accomplice to them in carrying such reports.

Nevertheless the rumours of intimidation had persisted around the town and district until that morning, with the debate just a few hours away.

That morning, too, the Gazette published a straw poll of councillors which suggested that if all members were at the council meeting, the vote would be so evenly divided that it could go down to the chairman's casting vote - and quoted the chairman, Rita Youngs as saying that if the votes were tied, she would not use her vote in that way and the application would fail - it would not be right or ethical for one person effectively to decide such an important application, and one which would have such far reaching affects on so many people in so many ways.

All these things played on Robin Anderson's mind as he set off from Bury St Edmunds, intent on getting to Lowestoft before the vote was taken. He had made up his mind at a very early stage, and once made up he was not the sort of man to change it. It was a decisive part of his character which he felt had stood him in good stead with his business dealings over the years, with one or two exceptions.

He would vote against the application. He lived near Bungay, knew the Common well, had walked there many times and enjoyed its peace and beauty, and felt that outweighed the acknowledged need for more housing - there were other sites in the district which could be developed, which were far less sensitive as far as environmental and historic interest were concerned, and they could also be developed more economically.

The road to Lowestoft, via Diss and Bungay, was a single carriageway route all the way, with many winding sections and few opportunities for overtaking. Robin knew he would not make the 7.30pm start of the meeting, but calculated that the debate would go on for at least three-quarters of an hour and perhaps more. If he could be there by 8pm, which he should achieve comfortably, he would be there in time to have his say, if necessary, and certainly be there to cast his vote.

It was a fine early October day, but dusk was well advanced as he headed out of Bury St Edmunds, passed the British Sugar Corporation factory, and along the short stretch of dual carriageway. A sports car passed him and then an old Ford Fiesta. The driver looked across at him and held his gaze, with a glare, for a couple of seconds as he passed, but he was not aware that his driving had inconvenienced him.

Robin drove his silver BMW through Great Barton and Stanton and out towards Wortham. The traffic was light and he was making good time along the straights, and driving sensibly but over the speed limits through the villages, taking in the beauty of the twilit evening, the lights bright in the windows of the thatched cottages dotted along the route, in the farms and in the churches. Tesco and Bernard Matthews lorries went in either direction, builders' vans, Green King brewery drays mingled with cars, and frustrated the more impatient drivers. One low slung Lotus had to cut in sharply in front of Robin to avoid an on-coming van as the driver overtook him and attempted to pass the vehicle in front of him as well - a pale blue Ford Focus driver by a pale blue-haired elderly lady driver.

Robin was not in the habit of sounding his horn at such drivers, but nevertheless he thought to himself: "A bit close! I don't need an accident now to stop me making the meeting."

The silver BMW had just passed a layby in Wattisfield, where the driver of the same shabby red Ford Fiesta was making a call on his mobile, and travelled 300 yards down a straight gentle slope to a left hand bend at the bottom. Robin was just thinking he had made good time as he turned into the bend, with his timed acceleration holding the camber as he curved out of it.

Without warning, out of what was virtually night, a dark coloured van shot across from an opening on his right, fast and accelerating, and swerved in front of the BMW. So sudden was it that Robin could scarcely turn the wheel to the left to avoid it when it struck him a firm, glancing blow, enough for the BMW's momentum to push it over the road and send it rolling over and over, down a short, steep bank before it crashed into a tree with a loud, sickening thud and tearing of metal. It came to rest five yards further on. Seconds later the vehicle burst into orange and black flame.

Robin Anderson was probably dead even as the dark van, with a screech of brakes and smell of rubber, accelerated off into the darkness, towards Diss.

CHAPTER FIVE

AT LOWESTOFT Town Hall, there was nowhere near enough room in the council chamber for all the public who wanted to hear what had been heralded in the press as the Outney Fen Decision debate. Around 200 people had gathered outside the building in the High Street, the old part of the town, carrying placards with slogans such as Protect Our Common Rights, Save our Fen, Don't Damage our Heritage, and Let Bungay People Decide. But although the demonstration was noisy, it was peaceful and orderly, much to Danny's relief. A meeting of the Save Bungay Fen Action Group had planned the demonstration, to leave councillors in no doubt about the strength of feeling among townspeople - they wanted the Fen, their fen as they saw it, left to its ancient and productive use as grazing land, a golf course, and as a playground for local children to enjoy. But it had to be peaceful - he was concerned that any uncontrolled activity, any aggression or intimidation of councillors as they went into the meeting, could damage their case.

Jenny was there with a photographer - two of a number of media people covering the meeting, including radio and television. The issue had captured the public imagination and had even been picked up by the national press, which saw it as reflecting a national dilemma in balancing the need for more housing to serve the growing population and the larger number of single families, with the protection of ancient sites of special historic and environmental interests - Britain's unspoilt landscapes.

Danny caught Jenny's eye and she came over to him.

"How d'you think the debate will go?" she asked. It was a question which came through friendship as well as her professional interest.

"Well, it's certainly going to be very tight. There seem to be very few people sitting on the fence," said Danny. "I've spoken to as many as I can, and with the survey you did in the Gazette which was pretty comprehensive, I'll be surprised if there is more than a couple of votes in it."

"If that," said Jenny. "The feeling that it could be a tie is one many are promoting. Certainly the Party activists are predicting that the chairman's vote could decide it. And I think you know she would vote against it."

"Maybe, but she's said she won't use her casting vote and that would mean the application fails," said Danny. "I'm - well, I don't want to tempt fate when something as vital as the Fen is at stake but..., well, I just feel we might do it."

"I don't think there are many members likely to change the views they already have - most minds are made up," Jenny agreed. "But you never know - it could hinge on just one mind being changed."

"Is there likely to be a full house - of members I mean?"

"As far as I know. Robin Anderson said he might not be here dead on 7.30pm, but he'll be here in plenty of time for the vote."

Jenny hesitated before moving off.

"I do hope you win this Danny, for your sake as much as anything. I know how much this all means to you."

"Thanks Jenny. And thanks for the support of the Gazette." And he smiled and squeezed her hand.

The public, including some still clutching their placards, were pushing their way through the entrance doors into the foyer and up the stairs to the council chamber. Danny followed. It was 7.25pm, and he was anxious to make sure he got a place before the doors were closed. He just made it, squeezing in at the back to stand in a confined corner with other protestors. He acknowledged those there he knew - Fenny Skipper was there among them, having managed to get a seat, and he noticed the development company chairman, George

Bell, and his agent, and a third man, suited and dapper, with glasses and a sharp face, who he took to be the company solicitor.

He had a good view of the councillors, seated along three sides of the tables set out in a square formation. One side, the top table, was still empty, soon to be occupied by the chairman, council solicitor, financial director, chief executive, committee clerk and monitoring officer. He counted 46 councillors - chairman Rita Youngs and Robin Anderson would complete the set.

Good, he thought to himself - there'd be no absentees, so no one could complain about the result of the debate.

Chief planning officer Tim Woodgate outlined the application, backed by slides of the plans and artists impression of how it would look. He was a man of average height, and though probably in his mid to late forties was completely bald, with just a low line of gingery professor hair linking each ear in a semi-circle round his lower head. He spoke quickly, and confidently, and went through the scheme in great detail.

Danny had to admit it looked very attractive, with a mix of houses - large detached executive homes, semi-detached family homes, tasteful terraces in tree-lined roads, groves and closes - a shopping arcade of 10 shops, play areas for children, the community centre designed to blend in with the homes, a beautiful linear park fronting the river for most of its length so families could sit on the banks and picnic in the summer, inlets to be constructed at two places in the river for the mooring of small boats, and two footbridges over the river, one at either end, for walking access to the villages of Earsham and Ditchingham. Tim Woodgate told the meeting that there were also plans to dredge the river and clear it of a build up of reed along its length around the Fen, and that a direct road access to the development from the bypass would be built at the developers' expense.

"There are issues to be resolved on some aspects of the design of the semi-detached homes, and of the types of tiles and bricks to be used," Mr Woodgate said. "The Environment Agency also has some concerns about flooding - a large part of the site is currently used as grazing meadows and is very low lying. Bungay people will know that it floods regularly in the winter. But modern technology incorporated into the design means the homes in the risk area will be raised and well protected.

"A geological survey will be needed on some parts of the site before work starts if the plans are approved - we have to bear in mind that there is an ancient plague pit on the site where the bodies of those who died in the Black Death epidemic were buried. Due care and respect has to be given to that even 500 years after it occured

"I have to emphasise that this plan does go against current planning guidelines as laid down by the Government - it goes without saying that this is a green site, an environmentally sensitive area of outstanding natural beauty containing some rare plants and creatures. The details of that have been well documented in the media over the past few months. Residential development is encouraged on brownfield sites, ones previously developed but currently derelict or lying dormant, and in ordinary circumstances we would be recommending refusal of the application."

Mr Woodgate paused before going on:

"But - and this is particularly relevant - the Government has announced quite recently that areas designated as of outstanding natural beauty need to be looked at again because they could prevent the development of sites so necessary in today's climate for housing...housing shortage that is.

"I have to say also that in Waveney, and indeed in Suffolk generally, there are few brownfield sites that have not already been developed. By its very nature this rural county has a much larger area of greenfield than most others in Britain. And the Government is now dictating that 58,000 new homes will need to be built in Suffolk by

2015 to meet the demand. Sites have to be identified for them.

"The advice we are now being given from central Government is that plans could be looked at favourably on greenfield sites in these circumstances, providing there is planning gain in terms of new amenities provided for the community, at the developer's expense, or a new road or road access schemes. Clearly there are both of these advantages in the proposals.

"Members have to balance all these things in making their decision. It is worth noting, also, that we believe the developers have not tried to cram too many homes on to this site - a fault we see in many smaller schemes put before us. This is a well thought out development, although as you will have seen and heard in the local media over the past few weeks, there is a big lobby that the environmental, botanical and historical assets of the land over which people claim to have had common rights for many centuries, override any housing need, however great.

"The planning department has looked at this very carefully and taken on board all the issues raised. We have also considered the public petition of 2500 names objecting to the scheme, and the many individual letters - over 200 in all. But on balance, and subject to the provision of the design amendments and the Environment Agency concerns being overcome, my department, on balance, is recommending approval. We had considered at one time making no recommendation, and it is a finely balanced issue, but that is our advice to members."

"It sounds as if they've been got at by the developers," thought Danny to himself as Tim Woodgate sat down. "They see it simply as a commercial site - they have no concern about its special character, its unique history, the famous names it meant so much to. And if building 2000 homes on such a beautiful land is not cramming them in, I don't know what is. One is too many - there has never been any building of any kind on the Fen in its whole existence except the golf clubhouse, and the pest house, which was only there for 50 years anyway."

Fenny was now on his feet, speaking as chairman of the Fen Wardens - interested groups were allowed three minutes to put over their views before members debated it. He chose his words carefully.

"My members believe that this is a remarkable scheme and one which, yes, has many advantages for the town. We respect the feelings of the townspeople and understand that they feel the Fen would be a big loss to them. But my members also question how many would actually miss it - a relatively small number, I doubt more than 200, use it regularly for recreation these days, no, for walking, or swimming, or flying kites. And though the golf club has 600 members, yes, many of them are from outside the town. Probably fewer than 500 Bungay people use it, and many of them not what you would call regularly. My members believe, yes, that set against the 10,000 or so for whom it would provide a much-needed home, the plan should be approved. Yes."

There were boos and calls of traitor from some members of the audience, and Rita Youngs had to warn them to be quiet. Danny felt sorry for Fenny, knowing what his personal feelings were yet having to put over the views of the majority of the wardens. The call from the public gallery would have hurt him deeply. Fenny continued:

"In the current climate it is becoming more and more difficult, yes, much more difficult, to let the Fen goings for grazing, even though it is good pasture. But the management costs are rising all the time. Yes, grazing is fully let at the moment, but we cannot see more than two years ahead with any certainty. My members want you to know that they have agreed to sell the Fen for development if the plans are approved. We are not disclosing the agreed sale price for obvious reasons, no, but it will provide the wardens with a dividend far is excess of anything they could hope for from the current use of the facilities there.

"Most members believe it is a good plan, yes, and the facilities it would provide for the town would far outweigh those it provides at the moment, and it would provide for many more people."

Fenny sat down, uncomfortably, clearly slightly embarrassed at what he had had to say - it does not rest easy on any shoulders having to express views you do not hold personally.

George Bell told the meeting why he felt the scheme would be such an asset to the town and district. He was a big man, tall, but still too stout for his 6ft, and had small dark eyes in a puffy face under ginger hair that was thinning and greying - just the sort of man, in his fifties, you would expect to head a big development corporation, Danny thought.

"Can I say straight away that we fully understand and appreciate the views of the people of Bungay. And we sympathise with them too," he began. "Outney Fen, and its Iris Glade - the name we are giving to this scheme - has been a familiar place to Bungayans since the town itself had its origins. But what our scheme will do is simply expand on that, add to the facilities and make them readily available to many more people. Yes, my company is in this to make a profit, but we also feel part of Bungay, and we are keen to enhance it, not detract from it. I love Bungay - I have visited it many times and grown to love it myself. I've enjoyed the Fen as it is, I've played the golf course. We will enhance the riverside amenity - you won't have to avoid stinging nettles and mole hills any more when we have landscaped the river banks..."

He laughed at what he probably saw as an effort to lighten the debate, but no one in the hall took it up, so he coughed dryly, and continued:

"... And the new community centre will be one the town can be proud of. I know the difficulties the town has had seeking grants to build a new one on the present site

- the one we will build for Bungay will incorporate all the facilities planned in that scheme and more. It will be the focal point of the whole development.

"We are more than happy to discuss the design details of the houses we build on the Fen, and amend them as necessary, and I thank Mr Woodgate for his comments that there are not too many homes on the site. Overall it is just over eight an acre - the standard these days for ordinary developments is twice that.

"Believe me, my company has a social conscience. We want to enhance the communities we build in, help the Government reach its targets, and help families acquire homes they desperately need at a price they can afford. I know your concerns, Madam chairman, on the length of the waiting list for homes in this area - this scheme would help to ease that considerably. I hope your members will allow us to do that."

There were more boos from the public as he sat down, breathing heavily and perspiring, with some people getting up and pointing accusing fingers at him.

"If you really want to do what Bungay wants then just get lost," said one voice, loudly. Rita Youngs had to tell them sternly that if that happened again the debate would be adjourned while the public were removed.

The Bungay Town Trust, once the administrative body of the town, now a charitable trust which had retained most of the civic assets when handing over power to the urban district council in 1910, was the largest single owner of goings on the Fen. The Town Reeve (Bungay was the only place in the country to retain that ancient office for the head of the trust), got up to say that the feoffees (the ancient name for members of the trust) were in a dilemma over the plan. They saw the Fen as it was as one of Bungay's finest historic assets, but a priority was making the most of their property from which profits were put to local charitable causes and projects in Bungay. So they had stepped back from supporting a proposal either way.

Rita Youngs again had to remind speakers to confine their remarks to planning issues - the district council could only make decisions on applications on planning grounds, not historic, nostalgic or emotional ones, however strong they may be.

After chamber of trade president Justin Proudfoot had expressed its support for the application on economic grounds - clearly it would be a huge boost to chamber members to more than double the number of potential customers for their shops and offices - Danny pushed his way through to the front of the public gallery area to speak on behalf of the action group, the last speaker before members debated the issue.

"Three minutes to talk about the Fen and what it means to Bungay people is not very long," he began. "I could eulogise for a day on it. But let me first say that the amenity aspects of the scheme are a smokescreen to a plan to turn our Fen - yes, ours, Bungay people's - into another modern housing estate, and that would be absolute sacrilege. It is such a special place to many people, for many reasons, and though you may talk about fewer than 200 people using it, the truth is that there can be very few people in Bungay that have not, at one time or another, been on the Fen, if only for half an hour or an hour. And the amenities this plan claims to bring - well, many, such as the improvements to the river, could be done readily, and the community centre will get built sooner or later, on the site of the present one - there are some very determined people working on that at the moment. It is very, very difficult to see any planning gain for Bungay people in this scheme at all. There would be a considerable and irretrievable loss to the town if Outney Fen is lost. I know there are many people who desperately need homes, but this is not the place for them - it is too big a price for any community to have to pay."

Danny paused. He had tried to keep his words as dispassionate as possible, and address the planning issues. But the council, if it did not know already through the media, had to know the strength of feeling that was against a plan that would change Bungay's character, landscape and atmosphere in many ways, for ever, and he told them that.

"This is no ordinary tract of green land - it has not served just as arable or meadow land all these centuries - it is a land of special historic interest," he went on. "Neolithic man settled here for a while, Bungay people took vital elements from the Fen in medieval times and later - flints, furze for their fires, shingle, turf, fruits, water and so on. And it has close links with famous people, such as French statesman Chateaubriand, who talks fondly of his walks there in his memoirs; painter Alfred Munnings got his love of painting horses when he visited the Fen - his paintings now sell for millions of pounds; and author Rider Haggard drew inspiration for his classic adventure stories as he wrote them in his study overlooking the Fen. You may say that is all in the past," he added, as he saw some members sigh and grimace, "but it is important to this town's heritage and this country's history. And besides, this is a beautiful site - no, not a site, that is a word that downgrades it to a simply commercial area - a beautiful part of our country which many people living today have fond memories of, and who want their children and grandchildren to come to have similar memories of. The action group…"

He was interrupted by Rita Youngs: "I'm sorry. We welcome your comments, but you have already gone well over your three minutes. We must now give councillors the chance to debate this vital application which has many wide ramifications."

Danny hesitated, then sat down reluctantly, to applause from the public gallery which brought another stern warning from the chairman.

The debate by members elaborated, to a large extent, on comments which had already been made, both for and against the plan.

"There is no doubt that this marvellous scheme will prove the making of Bungay. This town is decaying, its shops are closing, there is a lack of a proper community centre, and the town has to look to maximise its assets. The Fen is one of them" - that from Barry Halford, a Lowestoft councillor.

"The improvement to the river I have called for for a long time - it has been neglected for years, and it is becoming impassable in places even for rowing boats and canoes. This scheme will see it properly maintained and managed, and it will be a huge shot in the arm for tourism for the town," said Maxwell Redwood, one of Bungay's representatives. "We must bite the bullet and give this plan our wholehearted support. I know there are some people who don't like it, but for heaven's sake let's spare a thought for those in need of homes in this district and this county. I do feel the antis are being rather selfish in their opposition."

As he sat down and the next speaker stood up, a clerk came through from the ante room with a written message for the chief executive. He read it and immediately looked concerned, whispering urgently in the ear of the chairman, who looked startled and shocked at the message conveyed. But after whispering a return message she let the debate continue.

Danny noticed that George Bell exchanged meaningful glances with his agent and solicitor.

Marcus Gowen was speaking, vociferously, in favour of the application.

"I have been saying for a long time that the river at Bungay is an asset with a potential that is far from being fully realised," he said. "It has been sadly neglected in recent years. There was once a family picnic site at what was known as The Train Bridge - families sitting on the bank in the summer and watching their children paddling and play with their fishing nets. The scheme would bring that back, and bring many more people to enjoy boating on the river as well, once reeds are cleared and the bed dredged. I would be prepared to move that this application be approved, subject to the matters mentioned by the chief planning officer."

Simon Andrews was quick to second the proposal.

"There are many advantages this scheme would bring, not only to Bungay but the wider community, in addition to the much needed homes. It would be a flagship development for Waveney and Suffolk, and it is wrong to say people won't be able to enjoy walking by the river if it goes ahead. Clearly they will. What is more, we employ our planning department of professional people to guide us and advise us, and too often we don't go along with their recommendations. This is one major scheme on which we should accept their professional advice."

Several speakers from all political parties and none got up to offer their views, some for, some against, to a background of murmurings from the public gallery, though no more booing and applause. It added to the feeling that the final vote would be very close and there was a certain tension and buzz in the air.

Danny was getting anxious for another reason. He leaned over from his confined position and managed to tap Fenny on the shoulder.

"Where is Robin Anderson?" he mouthed silently. The debate was going on longer than expected. It was nearly half past eight. The 48th member of the council should have been there by now.

Fenny managed to gesture with a shrug and the shake of his head that he had no idea, and was equally concerned. He shared Danny's view that there could be only one or two votes in it, and with an odd number of members there, there would be no need for the chairman's casting vote, unless there were abstentions. It was vital that Anderson should be there.

Jason Gayzor, another of the Bungay representatives, was speaking. He was a good local politician and he put the case against the application eloquently.

"So Madam chairman," he said in his final sentences. "from a planning point of view this scheme is strategically wrong, from a community point of view, bearing in mind the controversy over the ownership of the Fen debated 40 years ago, it is ethically wrong, and there are few people in Bungay, in Waveney, in Suffolk indeed, who would not consider it environmentally wrong. Any planning application of this magnitude must bring some advantages to the community over and above those that could be achieved otherwise. This grotesque scheme does not - it simply steals from the town its most natural and best loved asset - our beautiful Fen, a haven, a retreat from the rigours of the day - work, school, household chores - an area for everyone to enjoy recreationally, unchallenged, provided they treat it with respect. It is the right of Bungay people to be able to continue to enjoy it. On behalf of them I beg you, I appeal to you, not to take away that right in favour of a scheme that gives nothing back."

Jason Gayzor sat down to the loudest applause yet from the public gallery. But with that being the last speech before the vote was taken, Rita Youngs let it go. But her final words sent concern through everyone involved with the Bungay campaign.

"Before we vote on the application can I remind members that they must make the decision on planning grounds and planning issues alone. Inevitably and understandably there has been some emotive talk tonight, but you do have to try to detach yourself from that."

She paused before saying: "I have to tell you, sadly, that Robin Anderson hasn't made it to the meeting. We have had a message that he has been involved in a road accident on the way here. That is all we know at the moment. There are no details of his injuries but we understand he has gone to hospital. I'm sure we all send our best wishes to him.

"Now councillors, I put the motion to you that this planning application be approved subject to the matters outlined by the chief planning officer, and as proposed by Mr Gowen and seconded by Mr Andrews. Those in favour please show."

The vote was by hand and many went up. Danny, from his position at the back, with an obscured view, could not see to count himself, but the chief executive, after a careful count, announced:

"Twenty-four for the motion. Those against?"

Hands were raised again, but it meant little and there were already loud whispers and concern among those there as they realised the application had been approved, before: "Twenty-three against the motion. The motion is carried," the chief executive announced.

So Robin Anderson's attendance would have been vital - the difference between success and failure for the campaign to save the common.

Danny stood stunned as the meeting broke up amidst sudden loud chatter, groups discussing animatedly here and there, the high ceiling council chamber full of a hubbub of noise and movement in contrast to the seated debate of a few moments ago.

Members of the media moved to get comments from key players in the scene, and George Bell exchanged handshakes with his agent and solicitor.

Coastal Radio were the first to get to him for a comment on air.

"Your re-action to that discussion and decision?"

"I'm delighted, absolutely delighted! And can I say straight away we will not let Bungay down on this. I am confident we can allay people's understandable fears and provide a development which Bungayans will come to appreciate as one of its finest assets.

"When will work start? Too early to say exactly, but we want to start as quickly as possible. We are sinking £400 million into this and shareholders will want to see an early return on that investment. And people will want to enjoy the many benefits of the facilities."

Listening nearby, Danny felt disgusted.

"He's taking the Fen away from Bungay people, but he won't let them down. What a hyporcrite," he seethed to himself.

He moved to speak to Fenny, who was looking somewhat forlorn, still in his chair, but he felt a hand on his arm. It was Jenny.

"I probably don't need to ask, but can you give me your thoughts on the decision for the Gazette?" she said, sympathetically.

"Jen, Jen you're right - you don't need to ask. I'm devastated, and so will be the majority of Bungay people. They are taking away the town's back garden, its residents' back garden, its finest asset, and what for? For greed. I hope the Fen Wardens can sleep soundly in their beds after this…"

He sighed heavily, and went on…"That may sound harsh - they are only doing a good commercial deal from their point of view, but it is not too many years ago that they promised it would always remain open for Bungay people to enjoy as a common.

"When I first heard of this plan - I think it was you who told me, wasn't it? I was angry, but simply didn't believe it would reach this stage. Where we go from here I don't know."

"Objections to the plan are likely to lead to a public inquiry. This is not the end of the planning process, though admittedly tonight's decision is a huge one," Jenny said. "What is your view on an inquiry?"

"Of course we will object as a group and have our say at the inquiry - we'll make sure there is one." Danny tried to sound more defiant than he felt. "And we will try to expand the support we have and seek new arguments against it. But I'm beginning to feel that money is talking louder than we ever could… Incidentally, any more news of Robin Anderson?"

"He's dead, Danny."

"Dead? He can't be. Dead? What happened? Rita Young's said…."

"I know. She had her reasons no doubt. But there was a hit and run accident on his way here. His car was shunted off the road, hit a tree and burst into flames. An awful business. Police aren't saying much more at the moment."

Danny felt the blood drain from his face. He felt sick. Robin had been a firm supporter of their campaign and the first name down when they were trying to gauge who would vote against the scheme.

"He's really dead? A hit and run?"

"There'll be an appeal for information on the driver who hit him, but nothing yet on the car. No one may have seen it."

"What a night. What a dreadful night...I'm going home." He paused, and squeezed Jenny's arm, and added: "Thanks for all you've done anyway, Jen."

"The Gazette will continue to focus on the issues, and you know I'll do what I can personally, Danny. This is not over yet by any means."

CHAPTER SIX

NORMALLY it took three minutes to walk from one end of Earsham Street to the other. But that day it took anything up to 20 minutes to patiently push your way through the huge throng of people trying to move in both directions and across, hampered further by those gathered round the stalls and coloured awnings lining both sides of the wide thoroughfare.

It was the day of the annual antiques street market organised by Bungay Chamber of Trade, an event full of colour and characters and bustle and chatter and noise, of the flute playing music student busking in front of Cork Bricks, of zany street entertainers, of hubbub with the occasional shout towards a relative or old friend some distance away in the crowd, the sizzling of the hog roast as queues lined up for their pork rolls and relish on the corner of Chaucer Street, others queuing at the Parravani's ice-cream van, people moving in and out of shops and pubs and restaurants, others calling for space as they tried to manoeuvre their sometimes bulky purchases…

This was an event which annually brought up to 20,000 people into Bungay from far and wide, to join townspeople and to fill Earsham Street and the adjoining Castle Meadow, linked to the street via the White Lion Yard, and where overflow stalls were set up in the shadow of the Castle. Over 100 stalls in all came from a wide area of south-east England to put their wares on show - china, furniture, books, old garden implements, ornaments, flags, pictures, military collections, glassware, postcards, miniature items, records, gramophones and just plain bric-a-brac in bulging cardboard boxes were all there to tempt the bargain hunters and collectors.

Earsham Street, with its old buildings and Dutch gables, lent itself well to the atmosphere of such an event, and many people went just for that - to be there for a day out, have a look round, have a drink in the King's Head Hotel or Three Tuns or White Lion, or a meal at one of the restaurants. It was at any time a vibrant street, with a variety of shops - one which had been almost re-born over the previous 25 years, a trend which the name of one shop there, New Beginnings Florists, seemed to encapsulate with its own brightness and the colours of its merchandise.

This year, though, other things were happening there to add to the intrigue of the event. Both side in the Iris Glade debate had their teams of campaigners there to lobby for support and press their case. Both had set up stands there. The Save our Fen brigade had banners adorning theirs, the volunteers wore T-shirts with the slogan on, and they encouraged people to add their names to the petition against the plan. Many did, though it proved difficult among the jostle of the crowds against the stand. The volunteers, some more aggressive in their approach than others, also had leaflets outlining the reasons why they felt the Fen should remain as it was. Small children had dressed as rabbits, otters, mice or owls and helped with the leaflets. Periodically they would stop in their lobbying to chant their pleas, through slogans and a catchy song which could just about be heard above the considerable incidental noise the market generated.

Pilgrim's stand was inevitably more substantial and grandiose, and one on to which people were invited to enjoy a glass of wine and talk about the scheme, what it would mean to Bungay, the homes and facilities it would provide and the many fringe benefits it would bring. Their brochure outshone the campaigners leaflets in size, glossiness and comprehensive content, with artists impressions of aspects of it, details and styles of the homes, the projected timescale of the project if it got the final go-ahead.

It went further - people were invited to enter a free draw included with the brochure in which the lucky winner would win one of the first homes to be built there. It was the sort of publicity stunt the company could afford, and inevitably it made people stop, read and think seriously about it, as members of the staff mingled with the crowds to hand out copies of the brochure to market visitors, wherever they were from.

Even so, many of them were quickly discarded and trampled underfoot, along with the inevitable proportion of Save Our Fen leaflets.

Danny was at the SOF stand just after lunch to do his stint with the volunteers, to help to encourage people to sign the petition and talk to those who wanted to know more. With some of the team having visited the pub over lunch spirits were running high, and the same went for the Pilgrim's staff whose stall was 50 yard away on the opposite side of the bubbling street.

It was not too far for some of the more aggressive members of either team to begin loud cat-calling - the Pilgrim's team helped considerably by a loud hailer that seemed to be produced from nowhere. At first it was all light-hearted, but as the lunch-time imbibing began to take full effect it became more personal, more aggressive and more nasty. The crowds milling around between the two stands found it all rather fun and entertaining - some of them even began to join in with the veiled accusations as they began to fly in either direction with ever-greater energy and venom. What had begun with a couple of voices shouting from either side became a cacophony as more joined in. Fists began to be shaken and fingers pointed. The mild repartee quickly became more sinister.

Danny tried to reason with his campaigners as he realised that the situation could develop into something which could do considerable harm to their cause. From the start he had always argued that their efforts should be strong and determined but at the same time peaceful and reasoned. But they ignored him. Their fire had been stoked and it was not to be dampened so easily.

It was not clear from which direction the first missile flew - it seemed to be the remains of a hog dog screwed up in the paper serviette that came with it, and it landed somewhere in the crowd. But it immediately increased the volume of shouting between the two stands and within a few seconds more missiles - coins, pencils, more half-eaten food, empty beer cans, cartons, sticks and even a trainer shoe were directed at the rival stands, many of them falling short and landing on those trying to enjoy the market.

When the missiles ran out, male members from the two sides angrily pushed their way through the crowds towards the other's pitch, meeting somewhere in the middle of Earsham Street. A melee quickly developed, with some of the crowd joining in and others panicking and screaming, either in fear or to tell them to stop as they struggled to get distance between them and the two forces.

Blows were exchanged, and as the fights and shouted accusations increased many in the crowds drew back and made their way from the market, back to the cars or their homes.

The urgent sound of a police vehicle was soon heard. When it appeared, blue lights flashing, officers in protective helmets and armed with batons piled out and quickly made the way to the centre of the fracas, pulling the antagonists apart as best they could.

Fortunately they had to use little force. Their appearance seemed to startle the campaigners and company subordinates whose enthusiasm had spilled over into outright physical antagonism, and they ceased their fighting with a minimum of protest and no aggression towards the police.

Nevertheless, the damage had been done, physically to some combatants from both sides who sported bloody noses, bruised faces and a few black eyes, but more critically to the reputation of the Save Our Fen campaign. That would be affected far more than those promoting the building project, Danny thought, as he surveyed the scene with dejected dismay.

He had remained on the periphery of the action, vainly trying to tell his team to step back from fighting, to walk away. He was aware of the shocked comments of some nearby stallholders and visitors to the market as they withdrew from the battle area, and he knew there would be inevitable repercussions from the incident.

As he completed the task of encouraging his campaigners to call it a day and dismantle the stand, with the crowds having melted away at an alarming rate, he saw Jenny making her way towards them, concerned on her face.

"What on earth has been going on? I've just heard a message on the police media voice bank about a pitched battle.

"Don't ask, Jen - don't ask," said Danny, disconsolately. "This is the worst thing that could have happened. This had meant to be a great opportunity to promote our cause and our case to the wider public and get them behind us. They won't want to know after this."

"After what, Danny - tell me what happened. How did it start?"

Danny started to explain, but he had not got very far when he was rudely interrupted by the Pilgrim's manager who had been in charge of their stand.

"Are you from the Gazette?" he asked angrily. "Yes? Well I want it on record that it was this lot who are responsible for this mess. We came here to let people know in an orderly way what our scheme was all about and these campaigners were intent on spoiling it. They started throwing missiles at us, and all we did was defend ourselves - put that down in your notebook. This has done your cause no good at all Mr Tegerdine, no godo at all -I'll make sure of that."

"Yes, OK Mr Finch, I'll give you a ring later to get your comments. Give me a little while," said Jenny in a businesslike way.

But Albert Finch had scarcely left with a scowl on his face when another man, his countenance just as grim, strode up. It was chamber of trade president Justin Proudfoot.

"What the hell have you done?" he almost shouted, confronting Danny. "I hope you're satisfied. In a few minutes of madness your herd has just ruined one of Bungay's most successful events and probably ruined the reputation of Bungay itself throughout the country. You promised me this would be a peaceful presence, and then you contrive a riot."

Almost without drawing breath, he added: "Don't expect any, any support at all in future from me or the chamber. We supported the Fen project in principle but a lot of members have a lot of sympathy for your cause too and were ready to negotiate. At least they had until now. This mess could see the end of our street markets and I hold you responsible for that Mr Tegerdine."

He strode off as abruptly as he had arrived, without waiting for any reply from Danny, who looked despairingly at Jenny and shook his head slowly.

"This has been a complete disaster - they're both right. Where this leaves the campaign now I don't know…Come on - you'll want a statement from me too no doubt. Let's do it over coffee at the Castle Visitor Centre."

He took Jenny's arm and they walked through the street where all the stalls were beginning to pack up and street entertainment has ceased. As he passed one of them a man called to him:

"Hey, do you still want this book mate? It was you interested in it wasn't it, this old thing about Bungay? I'm packing up after all this kerfuffle. It's yours for a couple of quid and I'll throw in the box of junk it was in."

Danny was scarcely aware of what the chap said, but he murmured assent and handed over £2 as he took the box and tucked it under his arm.

Danny didn't have to open the Gazette the next morning - it was all over the front page, with graphic action pictures of the incident. The staff photographer's routine visit to the event had co-incided with it and he had gleefully recorded it.

The story's prominence was inevitable, given the coverage the ambitious Iris Glade project and the determined opposition to it that had gone before. It was the sort of running story newspapers, radio and television relished, and this was a new twist which was sure to sell papers and attract visitors and listeners. Jenny had warned him that it would get wide coverage, and her professional integrity would not allow her to downplay it for Danny's sake. And she was not responsible for the headlines:

Melee Mars Market - Thousands flee as Fen campaign takes ugly new turn - three arrested.

The report itself was well balanced, with Danny's comments there among the others. He had tried to retrieve what he could from the situation.

"We had planned this as an opportunity to reach a wider audience of people with our campaign and invite them to sign up to support it," Mr Tegerdine said. "This was the last thing we wanted to happen and on behalf of the SOF action group I would like to apologise to all those whose enjoyment was destroyed by the incident, all those stallholders who had their day's work cut short, the chamber of trade, whose continued efforts to bring people into Bungay were clearly blighted by the incident, and to those innocent people who may have been caught up in it and possible hurt.

"It should not have happened, but I refute the suggestion that it was started by the campaigners - there were two sides in this and both must take equal blame. I hope Pilgrim's see fit to apologise in the same way.

"It was regrettable, but it must not lessen our campaign to fight for the future of Iris Glade and Outney Fen - they must remain as they are for the people of Bungay to enjoy, and we will continue to work towards that and oppose the scheme in a determined but responsible way."

Pilgrim's comments did not carry the same overt apology - George Bell took the opportunity to have another dig at the campaign, calling the incident "an example of what can happen when zealots jump on a band-wagon and take to using force as their superficial arguments against constructive progress and facilities which will make the community a better place are seen to have little substance."

In the following days the letters column of the Gazette was full of criticism of what had happened at the street market. Some writers said they could no longer back the campaign as a result, and even those still behind it said it had weakened the general resolve. One reader wrote to say an incident brought about by high spirits and initially harmless banter should not detract from the need to carry on the fight for the Fen to remain as it was; but letters with that message were far outweighed by the others.

The Save Our Fen group held an urgent meeting at The Fleece Hotel to hold an inquest into the incident at the street fair. Danny tried to read the riot act to the 15 there - a varied group of mainly ordinary citizens who genuinely had Bungay and the future of the Fen at heart. But it was not his forte - he had always seen the campaign as a positive, peaceful and common sense approach opposing the Iris Glade project in a constructive way with cogent arguments which the group aimed to regularly put before the public at every opportunity. The street market had been one of those opportunities, but it had gone badly wrong and harmed the campaign, there was no doubt about that.

Most at the meeting accepted that and debated ways and means of retrieving the situation. But Ben Cornthwaite voiced a more aggressive view.

"Look, we just can't go pussyfooting around this if we really feel strongly about it - I don't blame them that threw things at the Pilgrim stand at all. Sometimes words aren't no good, you've got to have action, let people see how you feel. Yes, words may sound good but do people really understand how we feel? No, that they don't - they want to see action - they want to see that we can fight for what we believe in," he said in his Suffolk accent.

"I was there and I for one don't apologise at all. I'm prepared to fight and there are others who'll do the same an' all."

Ben was around 45 and had been the voice of physical battle on the committee all along. He felt the same about the campaign as the rest of the committee but was at odds with most about how to achieve it.

He took a sip of his beer from the glass in a hand part-covered in his fingerless gloves which he seemed to wear whatever time of year it was, and went on:

"And let me tell you another thing - Pilgrim's aren't bothered by these peaceful words and reports and people signing petitions - they've seen it all before in other parts of the country and it hen't stopped them building there has it? Their board will be sitting laughing into their whisky at the feeble efforts the people of Bungay are making to stop them getting permission. If it was up to me I'd have less talk and more action."

"Ben, believe me when I say the fight at the street market did our cause no good at all and played into their hands. We've got to be strong but not physically aggressive, and anyway its not Pilgrim's we've got to convince about our case, it's the planners and now the Government inspector. They make the decision, not Pilgrim's, so what's the point in fighting them? We have just got to have faith in what we believe in and continue to let the world know why we believe in it and why we believe the Fen as it is is important and significant enough to be discarded as a site for thousands of homes, however much they are needed.

"That is what we have been doing and that is what we must continue to do, and Sunday's incident was a disaster for us and has set us back considerably. We have got to make up ground again, re-establish our reputation - and that is going to be a big task in which we all need to pull together. Will you pull with us Ben? We need you - we need everyone."

But Ben, a small man with small eyes in an earnest face, a wiry body with ill-fitting brown jacket, was not to be convinced. He stood up, took another draught of his beer and put the glass down with a thud on the table.

"No I'm not with you, Mr Tegerdine. We've tried the gently, gently approach for too long and it doesn't seem to have got us anywhere at all. Sooner or later someone has got to show these greedy developers that they can't just come and take our land just like that. No, they can't, and we've got to show them that - we've got to show them we mean business. But this committee won't do that - its got no guts, no spine. I've had enough."

And he put on his flat cap with two hands, and left the meeting, with close friend and ally Nobby Nobbs following him.

CHAPTER SEVEN

DANNY and the campaign committee, with the support of Jenny and the Gazette, continued to do all they could to keep it in the public eye. There was a march through Bungay, with 200 people carrying placards, culminating in a rally at the Butter Cross, an ancient, domed building, symbol of the town's heritage, erected following the Great Fire of 1688. Campaign stalls, raising funds to support it and with leaflets outlining the reasons for the opposition, were staged at as many local bazaars, fetes, exhibition and public events as possible, Names for the petition continued to be canvassed.

Pilgrim's response was to take out a full page advertisement in the Gazette and some regional newspapers outlining why they were having to look as greenfield sites in order to meet the Government's housing targets, and picking holes in the campaign arguments and the way it was being run. They and the district council, and the campaigners, prepared their cases for the inevitable public inquiry held by the Government's Planning Inspectorate.

And still the media carried more stories, locally and nationwide, of the need for more homes, of the relaxing of guidelines on sensitive areas, and highlighting often poignant individual cases which they said highlighted particular needs which were just examples of the general problem caused by a lack of homes.

Meanwhile, the Fen remained constant, through its autumn colours and gathered blackberries; it saw the sand martins migrate south again for the winter; people donned boots and scarves and warm coats and hats for their walks around the river; the Waveney ran dark and deeper and more rapidly, as melting snow from its upper reaches swelled it, until it spilled its winter water over its banks, flooding the Lows into a huge lake; well cocooned children played there, and when the flood water froze during a hard frosty period they skated on top of the shallow frozen floods, and their cheeks became flushed and rosy with the cold and their exertions and exhilaration; and they went home, reluctantly, in the dusk to a warm tea and cocoa and warm new-baked chocolate buns, and did their homework by the fire.

Spring came again, and the snowdrops around the site of George Baldry's house replaced the white of the frost, aconites peeped through, buds stirred on the silver birches in the curtain of Iris Glade, and the first sign of the leaves of the flag irises pushed above the water levels in the dykes. The skylarks sang, the owls resumed their sorties, the first cuckoo called across the Hards in mid-April. Nature's clocked ticked on, easily visible on the open Fen. But for how long?

"Danny? Are you there? What on earth's going on? What are your people up to?"

The phone had rudely awakened him from his slumbers at about 6.30am, and after a few seconds of getting his mental bearings Danny turned over and picked up the beside phone.

"Hello - whose that?" he asked croakily. "Oh, Fenny - what's the matter?"

"What's the matter is that someone has released all the cattle from The Lows and there are around 200 head of them clogging up the bypass - that's what's the matter," the Fen Wardens' chairman said agitatedly. "And it can only be your supporters who have let them out, Danny. I've been got up by the police and I've had to call out the farmers to try to round them up, but it's chaos down there at the moment."

"Oh, no!" Danny's dismay was obvious and he was fully awake. "But...how do you know it was our members?"

"Come on Danny- who else could it be? It's been done deliberately to cause more disruption. It's been done as another protest, same as that trouble at the street market..."

"Couldn't someone have left the gate open accidently?"

But Danny's hopeful inquiry was angrily rebuffed by Fenny.

"Accident? It's no accident when someone cuts through the locks to get them off. The gate of every enclosure has been deliberately opened and the cattle must have been herded towards the main entrance - there's very few left on the Fen. I'm not happy about this Danny - not happy at all. You know I sympathise with your cause but all this aggravation is testing my patience and it's not doing your campaign any good at all."

"I know, I know. But I can guarantee it is not the work of any members of our committee - they wouldn't do that. It must be someone else."

He paused, and then said:

"Look Fenny, I'll come down there now. I'm not sure there is anything I can do but I'll have a look."

Ten minutes later Danny was making his way through the Market Place and quickly saw that Fenny's word "chaos" was not exaggerated. Turning into Broad Street he saw early morning traffic mingling with cattle which had strayed even from the bypass towards the town centre. Angry motorists were sounding their horns and shouting at those trying to round up the cattle.

And when he got down to the bypass, the situation was worse - there was more traffic there and more cattle, with the police attempting to hold vehicles back while farmers and their men attempted to coax the animals back towards the Fen. With vehicles coming to a halt along the stretch of road, that was not an easy task as the cattle - mainly bullocks - were nervous from the sound and hubbub of sounding horns and shouting drivers, and tried to run in any direction.

If Danny was in any doubt about who was responsible for the disruption, is was dispelled by a sign in the middle of the bypass round about. Scrawled amateurishly on a large placard stuck on a post there was the message: *Fenmen: stop this plan or your cows will suffer.*

It was a chilling threat. Clearly someone or some group felt causing public disruption was the way to head off the Iris Glade scheme - people who had nothing to do with the town's campaign. But that would be tarred with the same brush by Pilgrim's and the Fen Wardens.

He spotted Fenny, standing by the main gate to the pasture and went over to him. His face was like thunder - it was unlike the usually mild-tempered man he had a lot of respect for.

"See what I mean?" Fenny almost shouted as he approached. "This is deliberate, absolutely deliberate. The campaign has lost any sympathy it had from me let me tell you."

"I understand that Fenny. This is awful and I'm so sorry it has happened. But be assured it was nothing to do with our committee - we have pledged not to be involved in any aggressive or disruptive action. This is the work of others - people jumping on a bandwagon, people who cause trouble for trouble's sake I guess."

"Well look over there, see? Ben Cornthwaite and Nobby Nobbs - they're on the committee aren't they? I'll guarantee they've got something to do with this."

Danny's heart sank as he saw the two men over the other side of the bypass, near the entrance to Clay's bookprinting factory where both worked, chatting together and looking self-satisfied. Fenny could be right.

He spotted someone else walking briskly down the street towards them - it was Jenny. How did the press miraculously appear at incidents as if they had inbuilt radar for them?

But he was pleased to see her - she looked more beautiful than ever in the glow of morning light, he thought.

He saw her stop and talk to Ben and Nobby, and jot down notes as she did so. Danny tried to make his peace with the troubled Fenny and then made his way towards her. They met in the middle of the roadway roundabout - nothing was moving, except the restless cattle as men continued their efforts to herd them, and it was perfectly safe.

"Hi, Jen - bright and early as always," he greeted her, and kissed her on the cheek. "What did those two have to say?"

"They reckon they saw cattle coming off the Fen when they arrived for their 6am shift, and called the police. Then they attempted to herd them back on to the meadows but it was an impossible task. They're not on the campaign committee now are they?"

"No, left last year. They're trouble-makers. I'm sure they've got contacts with the sort of people who relish taking aggressive action, whatever the cause. Fenny reckons it was them who cut the locks on the gate and let the cattle out."

"It was definitely deliberate then? They didn't say anything about that. Fenny could be right - I'd better talk to him."

"Well, be careful - I haven't seen him worked up like this before, but I guess the whole thing is getting to him. Can't be easy being the chairman of the Fen Wardens at the moment - they are probably the most unpopular group in the Waveney Valley. He's blaming our campaign, and it's going to be difficult to dissuade people from that view. But you can tell your readers from me that it categorically was nothing to do with the committee and we distance ourselves from any disruptive action."

Danny sighed heavily again.

"I don't know - since all this started I seem to have spent half the time apologising for things that are nothing to do with me or the campaign group. It's getting in the way of getting across our arguments for retaining the Fen as it is. This sort of thing is just not helpful - we don't want to lose the popular support."

"I think most people are still behind it, and so is the Gazette. Look, I must go and find Fenny. Shall we have coffee at the Earsham Street Café later - 12.30ish?"

"Yes, let's do that. See you there."

Once again the Gazette had the issue on its front page, with pictures of the chaotic scenes on the bypass under the heading: *Cattle Chaos at Bungay. Campaign committee accused by angry farmers.*

THE campaign to stop Bungay's Outney Fen being developed took a new twist yesterday as cattle were deliberately released on to a busy main road.

The incident caused considerable chaos on the town's bypass and in the town for rush hour traffic, and Fen Warden chairman Fenny Skipper angrily accused those campaigning against the £400 million housing scheme of being responsible.

It was two hours before the last of the frightened animals could be coaxed back on to the Fen. But a campaign spokesman insisted it was nothing to do with them and blamed agitators keen to cause maximum disruption.

And so it went on. It was a balanced report, which also included news of the latest activities planned by the campaign committee, but as Danny read it it was clear to him that it represented another knock to the backing for their efforts. Why was it that so often, wherever it was and whatever the cause, troublemakers moved in under the guise of supporting it? It only played into the hands of the developers.

The report also included a section on the planning inquiry into the scheme, saying that a date had now been fixed for it.

Danny and Jenny talked about it again that evening as they walked, with Megan, on the Fen, through Iris Glade, and stood on their bridge in the April chill of the early evening dusk. The early cuckoo called, heralding another spring, and nature's burgeoning.

CHAPTER EIGHT

THE public inquiry was held at the Fisher Theatre in Broad Street, an historic building, part of Bungay's rich heritage, and recently restored to its original use for which it was built by the Fisher family in 1828.

That had been made possible through the determined efforts of a group of people who had a vision to make it a theatre again, for music and drama productions, art workshops and related uses, as well as for meetings.

It was an appropriate venue for this vital planning inquiry, Danny thought as he hurried through St Mary's Street, glancing at the Town Clock on the church instinctively as he did so - it was just chiming the three-quarter hour, just as it had done for 200 years.

"Nine forty-five - I'm in good time," he thought.

Time to have a chat with the lawyers representing the Save Our Fen action group. Danny had given notice that he wanted to speak at the inquiry, as had several others, including the Mayor, Sally Carter, a determined woman in her prime, who ran a gift shop in Earsham Street.

Yes, it was an appropriate venue, Danny thought. The Fisher Theatre was formed by a group of five people who had a vision to acquire the building, the only one of its kind left in the country, and return it to theatre use. There had been many setbacks, some seemingly irretrievable, but the society refused to give in, and eventually bought the building with the help of a loan, and set about raising funds for their ambitious scheme. Even then there were disappointments, hold-ups and frustrations. But they simply held their vision and their courage - and the result was a facility of which they could be proud, a testament to Bungay's spirit, and a building which had proved a great asset to the town, a living theatre and community venue.

It had been a theatre for only 16 years, and since then had had many uses in the past 160 years. For a long time it was Bungay's corn exchange, and many momentous meetings had been held there down the years, including one to battle against a plan to divert the River Waveney around Bungay, another against the extension of the river trade to Diss, and yet another against the unfair levy of church rates.

All were in the 19th century, and all had seen Bungay mentioned in Parliament and the national press. Now this building would see a meeting which could prove equally momentous, Danny thought, one which from the SOF point of view would leave people over a wide area, perhaps the whole country, in no doubt about the strength of protective feeling there was for the Fen, Bungay's back garden, its heritage, part of its own make-up.

There were several people walking through the Market Place, past the ancient Butter Cross and the Black Dog weather vane, as Danny reached there, and suddenly he could hear the sound of a chattering crowd, and raised voices. The scene as he turned into Broad Street took him by surprise.

A mass of perhaps 200 people had gathered outside the entrance to the theatre, many of them brandishing placards with message scrawled on them: Hands off Our Fen, Show Common Decency - Drop this Plan, and Build in Your Own Back Yard were among them.

They were the milder ones - others were more Anglo-Saxon, bordering on the obscene, in their wording, venting the anger and emotion of those brandishing them, as they stood glaring at those entering the building.

Something much more menacing caught Danny's eyes and ears. At the back of the crowd, trying to push forward, were a group of people he did not recognise, with hate in their eyes, shouting obscenities and threats at those they thought were among the developers and their team of lawyers and architects. They were clad in dark clothes, with long lank hair beneath woollen hats pulled down over their ears. Their voices were high and hating, almost snarling, and as he stood there, Danny saw one hurl something towards the theatre door. Fortunately, it did not hit anyone but the door itself, but it startled one of the developers' team and he stopped and glared grimly towards the crowd before going in.

A press photographer was taking pictures of the scene, and Danny spotted Jenny with notebook in hand. He made his way towards her.

"What's going on Jenny - we don't want this sort of thing. We wanted a peaceful demonstration, not another mob! Where did that lot come from?"

"I don't know - I'm trying to find out, Danny," she said. "All I know is that we had an anonymous call at the office this morning saying if we wanted to see some action, be at the theatre this morning. It was the same with the cattle incident. They've obviously been organised from somewhere. I'll let you know as soon as I find out more."

“It wasn’t Ben who made the call was it?” in a semi-sarcastic tone.

“No, I don’t think so - I didn’t recognise the voice.”

She smiled uncertainly at him, and moved away into the crowds. Danny, with a heavy sigh, made his way into the building, as the crowd moved in closer, with some hoping for seats in the public gallery.

He managed to find a seat in the packed auditorium, but by the time the inquiry opened, many were standing at the back and the doors had to be closed with many still outside. A number of the protestors had managed to get in, armed with their banners, and were making their presence felt, while the chanting crowds outside were clearly audible in the theatre.

But the Government inspector hearing the inquiry, Giles Watson, was experienced in his role, and made it clear that the inquiry would be tightly controlled, on his terms. He sat behind a table set out on the stage. Two other tables, slightly apart from it and at right angles to it on both sides, were occupied by planning officers, lawyers and company representatives, with the table filled with plans, maps, reports and the other paraphernalia that goes with a major planning inquiry.

The arguments followed largely the same lines as those at the public meeting and the council meeting earlier in the year, with the eloquence of the lawyers in their rejoinders with clients and planning officials often bringing laughter from the public gallery.

It was appropriate, thought Danny wryly, that the hearing was taking place in a theatre, such was the acting ability of some of those involved - it would be enjoyable were it not an issue so vital to the future of Bungay and its Fen.

Many people had asked to speak and some did so passionately, both for and against. But Pilgrim's boss George Bell was clearly confident that his plan would succeed.

"This region of eastern England will need another 58,000 homes in the next 10 years if current demands for housing are to be met, according to Government figures," he said. "Developing brownfield sites can only achieve a certain proportion of that figure - other sites have to be found, and that does mean using some greenfield sites.

"We are aware of the public views on this. When we look at sites such as Bungay Fen we are fully aware of our responsibilities to come up with a scheme that is particularly creative, sensitive to the environment and to the community, and enhances rather than detracts from the surroundings. We believe the Iris Glade project achieves that, retaining the character and the rural views, and providing Bungay with leisure and recreational facilities it could not hope to achieve on its own, while providing homes for hundreds of people who desperately need them.

"This project will be a credit to Bungay, of that I can assure you."

It sounded a plausible argument, but there were speakers against it who spoke with equal passion and some emotion as the inquiry moved into its second day. The whole theatre fell silent as one middle-aged resident, Amy Baldwin, clearly overcome at the thought of the Fen being lost, appealed to the developers.

"I want you to go down there, deep on to the Fen, at dusk. See what you feel. See how you are moved. See it as it is then, and imagine how it will look with the trees and the meadows and the cattle and the kingcup and the purple willow herb and the blackberries and the barn owls and the skylarks and the kingfishers, all those and more, stripped away and replaced by houses," she half shouted, her voice breaking.

"Go there at that time, and tell me what you feel, and tell me you are not moved by it, that it is not special, that it is not unique. That it is not a sacred place. Tell me that if you can.

"Two thousand homes you want to put there? The Vineyard House is the only one worthy to be part of that scene, part of that beautiful place. You tell me there are people who need homes to live in – but what are homes in this community worth if this Fen and all it stands for is no more.

" I am not a zealot. I am not an environmental campaigner per se. I am simply pleading for this beautiful place to be left untouched. You talk about areas of outstanding natural beauty, and environmentally sensitive areas. If those that drew up those guidelines were sincere then Outney Fen was exactly the scene they had in mind when they were doing it.

"But do you see it for its beauty? No, no – you see it in terms of the millions of pounds you could potentially make from it, don't you?"

Amy voice was rising with her passion and she was having difficulty keeping control as her feelings spilled out.

"You are driven by one thing – greed, and you are prepared to wheel and deal and sell your soul to get what you want and then move on to rob some other community of its heritage in the same criminal way. You are despicable pigs…pigs all of you, with your fat bellies and fat wallets and fat cigars. Your interest is not in giving people a home in a pleasant rural area, it is in conning their money out of them by making them believe that is what you are doing for them. How generous! How generous and big hearted you are! Look at your plans! Look at them! The chosen few will have a river view if they are lucky – the rest will be in the middle of a concrete and brick maze with a view of their neighbours' homes and washing lines. They might as well be in the middle of a city. And you have the nerve to call it Iris Glade! What a nerve! What an insult to the beauty that gave this place its name! Your high and mighty brief on what this place will be and what it will mean to people isn't worth the paper it is written on. It is meaningless. You might try to con innocent people out of their money, but you won't con me or any of us here."

The inspector tried to interrupt, but Amy was in full flow.

"Please, leave this sanctuary alone, I beg you! Please leave it as it is, as it has been enjoyed for hundreds of years by thousands of people. We will welcome anyone here to enjoy it with us, as it is – as it was made by God and nature. Please don't take it away. Don't dig it up. Don't ruin it. Don't break our community…don't break…our…hearts. Please, I beg of you…drop this awful plan…Please…"

The last phrases came out slowly, gulpingly, chokingly, her voice getting lower as the emotion came to the surface and finally she could no longer hold back the sobs that shook her whole body.

As ushers led her back to her seat there was momentary silence - then loud and sustained applause broke out in the theatre. The inspector called for order, and when the hubbub continued, he announced a 10-minute adjournment.

When the hearing resumed, the lawyers for the developers asked the inspector if he would allow an additional witness to be called to highlight the need for more housing. Mr Watson was not sure it was directly relevant to the inquiry, but he agreed after a pause.

A woman of about 25, with short brown hair with blond highlights and pointed features was ushered in to the witness box. Answering questions from the developer's lawyer, she said her name was Yvonne Delgardo, she was a single mother with three young children, and they lived with her mother in a two-bedroom flat in Beccles.

Her face seemed vaguely familiar, Danny thought.

During her evidence she looked nervous, kept her eyes down or looking around her, and frequently had to be asked to speak more clearly so she could be heard by everyone in the room.

Often speaking breathlessly, Ms Delgardo told a harrowing story of her life in the cramped flat, with she and her three children sharing one room, with the other occupied by her mother, and various male friends she brought home not infrequently from the pub.

She said she was high on the housing list but there had been nothing available for the past two years and there was little hope of a home for her and the children at the present time.

But she had managed to save some money, she had a good job, and she had been told that she may be able to get a mortgage to buy a small house for herself and her family, if there was any affordable housing available in the area.

"I love my mother dearly, but it's not no good for the children to be in that flat," Ms Delgardo said, in a voice which as almost apologetic. "It's not a good experience. They get woken late at night, there's bad language, rows, violence even, when she and her boyfriends get back drunk. Mum's always sorry in the morning and makes it up to the kids, and so I say, don't worry, they'll be OK, but I know in my heart they won't. They're getting bullied at school cos their friends heard about what goes on, and kids are cruel.

"I'm doing my best for them, but it's just not working. I..."

She sniffed and took a handerkerchief to her face as she began to break down, through nervousness and emotion.

"I... I look into their eyes, like, sometimes.... sometimes, and I see... see their confusion and... and hurt and sadness, y' know? My heart breaks up when I see them like that. They're good kids, they can do well, but....but they're losing out, like, and I can't seem to get anywhere for them....don't seem to be able to help them... help them to get them out of it, y'know..."

She wiped away more tears, took a deep breath in an effort to compose herself.

"I heard what that last lady said about the Fen and how beautiful it is, how much it means to her. But my kids are beautiful too, y'know - they're precious to me, and they're human beings, we're human beings, aren't we, y'know. Shouldn't they come first?"

Ms Delgardo cried again quietly, fighting to control it.

"I don't know what sort of home that lady's got, like but I doubt she's living in the conditions we are. I don't know anything about planning...and land...and what ought to be built where. All I know is that my kids desperately need a home of their own, and I can't give them one and I feel...I feel so helpless...there's no one to do anything to help people like me. I've tried everything...everything, everywhere, but I can't see the sunshine ahead...only clouds, only dark, and rows, and fighting for space in a depressing, overcrowded pit. I can't...I can't...I can't..."

But she choked on whatever she was going to say, and put her head in her lap, and wept pathetically.

Uncomfortable murmurings rippled through the public gallery as she sat there in lonely desolation.

It was Mrs Baldwin who moved forward to her aid and helped her, comfortingly, caringly, consolingly, out of the theatre - protagonists united by human feelings.

As they left, the developers lawyer, was on his feet, addressing the inspector:

"Sir, we have had an emotional morning, but I make no apologies for bringing Ms Delgardo before you. She is one woman, one mother, urgently in need of a proper home for her family. But her's is not an isolated case by any means. We brought her before you today because she represents many thousands of people, particularly young families, in a similar situation - those without a home of their own, living with in-laws, living in cramped or sub-standard conditions, probably in this town, certainly in this county of Suffolk, and undoubtedly countrywide.

"She is a prime example of why the Government has set housing targets for local authorities. They may seem high - 58,000 in this region alone as you've already heard - but they represent the national need. And she is a prime example of why companies like my client Pilgrim are urgently pursuing planning permissions for sites we would not otherwise consider, because of their environmental excellence.

"My client puts forward this plan for Bungay Fen reluctantly, but they believe there is a compelling argument for this housing scheme which will benefit this community in many ways - and will fulfil the not unreasonable dreams of people like Ms Delgardo, a devoted mother and hard worker who as you have clearly seen is at the end of her tether in her efforts to find her children a home - not a luxury home, not an expensive home: simply a humble home of modern standard they can call their own.

"We don't think that is too much to ask, and that is why we are inviting you, Sir, to back this scheme for Bungay which can also be seen as an example of what can be achieved by imaginative design in the interests of home seekers and the needs, social and recreational, of the local community in general.

"Yes, this scheme is a commercial enterprise. Yes, the Fen Wardens and my clients stand to make a hefty profit if its gets the planning go-ahead. But also: yes, it will provide people like Ms Delgardo with new hope and a vastly better quality of life in which her children will be better able to grow and flourish and learn to make a useful contribution in their adult lives."

The inquiry moved on, the inspector patiently listening to the arguments on both sides, receiving written statements and data, maps, plans and other paraphernalia that goes with the business of trying to come to a reasoned, objective conclusion on a sensitive and emotional issue.

But the pleas of the two women that morning were what remained at the forefront of the minds of most of those there, and it is they that were given most prominence by the media as they reported the inquiry in newspapers and on radio and television the next day. They made the headlines and the pictures as the media angled on their widely contrasting situations and hopes for the outcome. The picture of Mrs Baldwin's sympathetic arm around the still weeping Ms Delgardo made particularly poignant viewing.

CHAPTER NINE

IT TAXED Danny's mind too, as he went home after that day of the inquiry, collected Megan, and headed for the Fen. He needed to think about all that he had heard, to get into perspective the events of the day, and try to decide where the campaign and the future of the Fen stood.

It was dark, but not pitch dark, and he could make out the familiar path easily - the main one, which once led on to the Fen from the town over the railway level crossing, and was now the main public access off the bypass. After a day on her own Megan was eager for exercise, and ran ahead, disappearing into gorse bushes momentarily and then re-appearing, returning to Danny and circling round behind him, the shepherding instinct always there. The scrub oaks and silver birch trees were shadowy objects, looming out of the darkness beside the track as they made their way down the ancient land towards the furthest point of the river, beyond Iris Glade to the musky, magic tract of grass and fern and gentle river sounds. It seemed to shimmer in waiting, even in the dark.

Danny made for the bridge over the dyke and leaned on the rail, looking down into the dark water. Iris Glade and the town were ahead of him, mere vague silhouettes merging with the darkness, and the Vineyard House was away to his left. The only sounds were the occasional insect noises, a gentle splash from a fish surfacing, or an otter diving, the just audible rustle of a vole or some other creature moving through the grass on a night-time mission. Nature never slept completely.

How many times had he been to that retreat, he thought idly. How many people had he walked there with, from childhood to adult days? Running, playing, walking, talking, discussing, ambling, courting - whatever the activity, always enfolded in the Fen's relaxing, soothing, understanding, unchallenging, unaccusing demeanour. And if he had enjoyed those qualities, and cherished them, many more people must have done also, and would share his love of the place, and have many memories of it. It could not fail to leave a positive impression on anyone, and have a renewing influence on them. Surely no one could have negative feelings about the Fen itself, memories of it they wanted to blot out?

Or could they? Danny tried to rationalise, as the darkness closed in and Megan continued to sit patiently by his side, head as always cocked and alert, tongue out, patient, not flickering at the sound of a distant gun, somewhere beyond the Vineyard Hills, as a farmer, presumably, tried to bag a game bird, or rabbit.

Of course they could. He thought of George Baldry, a true countryman who had lived his life beside the Fen, and in a book on his life had recounted how his grandmother had wandered after a stray cow on the Fen late one evening. A fog had come down as she sought the animal, and she had become disorientated as the thick fog and darkness closed in.

She was found the next morning, lying huddled under a gorse bush, suffering badly from hypothermia, and died two days later, without uttering another word.

As a man of the Fen, a simple man yet full of rural knowledge and with a thinking man's mind, George Baldry would have grieved as badly as anyone at the loss and the tragedy and the terror and loneliness of such a death - but would not have been moved to hate the Fen and vow never to venture on it again, or anything like that.

But others might, Danny mused. What if someone had met a violent death there? Murdered at the hands of a jealous lover, or committed suicide there, or drowned in the river? Relatives with little knowledge of Outney, or affinity for it, may well curse it to the end of their days and never want to set foot on it. They might want to raze it from the face of the earth, to exorcise the painful memories.

And then there were the views of Mrs Baldwin and Ms Delgardo. Danny shared Mrs Baldwin's emotional defence of the Fen and her deep love of it. But he had been moved by the plight of Ms Delgardo, her concern for her family's welfare and future. Her concern would not be for the spirituality and beauty of the Fen - she would see it, and the plan for it, quite reasonably as a chance to better her children's situation, and there is little that can override a woman's innate protective instinct for her offspring. It would override any other concern, he thought.

In deciding the future of the Fen should that, ultimately, be the priority? Was it morally right to argue against human need?

"Meg, are we being selfish about this Fen thing?" Danny said out loud. "Are we looking at the full picture? Should we forget this whole campaign, let progress take its course…I don't know."

He stepped off the bridge and headed slowly through the visible dark towards the town again, through Iris Glade and the magical curtain of trees, with Megan padding just ahead of him.

"…trouble is, you love this unique and wonderful place with the same passion that I do, don't you, Meg."

Next morning, the day he was due to have his say at the inquiry, Danny went to the Fen early. It was a dank, overcast morning, with a heavy mist, not quite a fog, limiting the scene and shrouding the colour almost to monochrome, the gossamer cobwebs on the gorse highlighted by the burden of moisture, a testament to the strength of this most delicate of nature's creations.

The scene matched Danny's heavy heart. He had lain awake most of the night, the things he had heard during the day turning over and over in his mind, but he was unable to co-ordinate them and get them into perspective. Two women had spoken equally passionately, equally movingly in their contrasting ways of their different lives, different hopes, different emotions. His heart had gone out to Yvonne Delgardo and her intolerable situation, and Danny found it impossible to equate them in his fitful dozing and waking - the questions kept coming into his mind, but no clear answers would come.

Was it right to campaign for the Fen to remain as it was when there were people and families like Yvonne Delgardo so desperately in need of a home?

Was it right that a beautiful landscape which had remained virtually unchanged since time began and which Bungay people had come to call their own should be put to the bulldozer in the name of progress? What should be the overriding priority - which needs and desires should prevail?

Often a visit to the Fen would help to get things clear in his mind, but this time it was no help. The misty, damp atmosphere served only to fog and confuse his mind further, and as he trudged back towards the town he could not see through the mist, with Megan at his side, he shivered with the dampness, cold and the uncertainty that pervaded his brain.

Two hours later he arrived again in Broad Street to the familiar site of campaigners gathered outside the Fisher Theatre, still with their placards, some looking slightly tatty by this time, brandished determinedly. They knew Danny was to be speaking at the inquiry, and a cheer went up as he arrived.

"Go on Danny - tell 'em straight, tell'em to leave our Fen alone!" one urged.

"You can do it Danny - you're our Bungay man. We're right behind you," said another. And a third, somewhat less loudly:

"Thanks for all you've done Dan - you deserve to see the Fen saved. You'll do it - we're depending on you."

He paused and nodded to them, half smiled, but said nothing as he went through the double doors, through the foyer, past the box office and through into the auditorium, and took a seat three rows from the front, on his own. The comments he had heard outside had only blurred his thoughts further, and he sat back, staring ahead of him.

His eyeline focussed on the historic proscenium header which had been found during the initial clearing work in the early days of the project to restore the theatre to its original use. It had been found under the rubble and debris in the basement, had been restored as the best example of its kind anywhere in the country, and was now back in its rightful place above the stage. Its design was leaves and flowers, with a face in the centre, a childlike face with something of a wistful, appealing look on it, one which now stared back at him unflinchingly as he sat there.

It reminded him uncannily of the face of Yvonne Delgardo, and after a few moments he averted his eyes.

When the inquiry resumed the Save Our Fen campaigners were again in the theatre in large numbers to listen to the proceedings, as they had been each day. With the development company and the planning authority having completed their evidence the process of hearing others who wanted to speak had begun the previous day - the Fen Wardens, the town council, the chamber of trade and the Suffolk Wildlife Trust all made their views known directly to Mr Watson, and half a dozen private individuals who had asked to speak were given their chance - the last of them on this day, when Danny would speak for the campaigners. It was set to be the last day, with Mr Watson having indicated that he planned to conclude the inquiry around lunch-time and spend the afternoon visiting the Fen and its environs to see the situation first hand before going off to make his report.

Danny only half listened to those who went before him - there was little said he had not heard already, and he was still going over in his mind what he wanted to say, what he should say, what the campaigners who saw him as their spokesman were expecting him to say.

What would he say? Even as he heard his name called and he got up to go to the witness table, his mind was not totally clear.

"Mr Tegerdine - you wanted to make a statement."

"Yes Sir, thank you. I will try to be as brief as possible, but you will know already that there are widespread strong feelings against this plan.

"When I first learnt of the application to turn Outney Fen into a vast housing estate, I found it hard to believe - I simply couldn't understand why anyone would seriously seek to spoil this beautiful corner of our country, virtually untouched since people first settled in what we now call Bungay. The Fen is its back garden, its safety valve, its peaceful haven, its place to walk and play and picnic and think and muse. It has a place in the hearts of many, many people, and it contains a myriad of flora and fauna, including some rare species. During a single walk you can see families of swans and cygnets, kingfishers, barn owls, herons, even the occasional otter…

"You can hear the sounds of the river, enjoy its beauty and its relaxation. It is an unchanging part of the scene in a rapidly changing world. I thought when I heard of the plan what a tragedy it would be to see this heathland and grazing area bulldozed to make way for hundreds of homes and shops and concrete areas in the name of progress.

"You have heard some passionate pleas over the past two days on behalf of the Fen - pleas from the heart to leave it as it is, as an outstanding area of natural beauty. I identify with those views - I have enjoyed the Fen since I was a boy, fishing, swimming, playing football and cricket, making camps in the gorse, walking, running, and in more recent years appreciating its unique character, beauty and atmosphere, a spiritual place that inspires you and has inspired many famous people in the past. I could name some and go into why and how their work was fuelled by the Fen, but I don't want to take too much time."

Danny paused, trying not to gabble, trying to compose his thoughts, and his own emotions. He took a deep breath.

"I have fervently believed for years that the Fen, Bungay's common, should be left as it is for Bungay's people and anyone else who wants to enjoy everything it offers. I sympathise entirely with Mrs Baldwin's emotional plea, which came from her heart and reflected the views of many Bungay people - you will have seen an endless list of names on the petition which will be among your papers, sir. She spoke well. Her views, Bungay's views, must be taken into account.

"You also heard moving and compelling evidence from Ms Delgardo about her plight, her need for a home, her need to have a chance to make a better life for herself, her efforts in vain to find a home of her own, to get her and her children out of their intolerable situation. We're told there are not enough derelict sites to build houses on, that untouched rural green acres will have to be sacrificed by the ever-increasing need for homes - is it really 58,000 in Suffolk alone, will the Waveney Valley, Dedham Vale, the Stour Valley, have to be sacrificed?

"Sir…" Danny was clutching the table in front of him now "…I love our Fen so much. It is…my haven, my beautiful retreat…my… my inspiration I suppose…how could I let it go without a fight? What is the greatest need?"

There seemed to be an uncertain quietness take over the room as those there saw Danny clearly struggling with his feelings and remain in control.

"Since I heard the evidence of these two woman I have been agonising over this whole thing. Where is…where is the greatest priority? Is it to retain this precious example of…nature's creation, or is it to let it go for the sake of people like Ms Delgardo, who was so clearly…at…at the end of her tether and in such need of a home she can call her own so her children can flourish and grow in comfort and healthy surroundings?

"Am I...are we here, all these people...being, what...I don't know...yes, are we being selfish, in campaigning to retain this Fen land for us? If it was truly common land, is it for the common needs of people...such as homes?"

Danny took a deep breath, trying to compose himself, as he looked momentarily at the faces in the hall fixed on him, following his words in complete concentration, mesmerised. And he looked at the inspector, and then looked down at the table, scarcely; seeing it, clutching it tightly.

"I don't know...I just don't know what is right...what is best for...but...I'm sorry, I'm...so...sorry...but..."

Danny suddenly stood up straight and looked at the inspector. He hardly knew what he was saying, but suddenly he said it, firmly:

"I have to withdraw my personal opposition to the Iris Glade scheme, sir."

There was a moment's complete silence, then gasps from the assembled campaigners. As they took in fully what Danny had said - Danny of all people, who had been instrumental in forming the campaign to save the Fen - some stood up. There were cries of "Traitor!", "Judas!" repeated by several of them, and another called angrily: "How can you desert us like that," as Danny left his seat, and left the auditorium with the vitriolic accusations, reaching a crescendo of noise, ringing in his ears.

The inspector and ushers in the theatre called for calm and quiet, but in vain as the anger of many looked set to cause pandemonium. Danny stopped momentarily in the doorway and looked back, tears clouding his eyes, at the campaigners who had turned into an angry mob. And at the header above the stage.

Was there a wry smile on the face in its centre?

CHAPTER TEN

DANNY left the building and went straight home. Megan barked as he unlocked the door, and jumped up eagerly as he entered, but he was hardly aware of her as he sank down on the sofa, closed his eyes tightly.

He remained like that for some minutes, saying out loud from time to time:

"What have I done? What...have...I...done?"

He got up and paced around the house, trying to come to terms with the events of the morning. Had he done the right thing? His decision to withdraw his opposition had been almost instantaneous, and yet in his heart of hearts he knew the previous day that that was going to be his decision. The needs of people like Yvonne Delgardo made him feel that they should come before any romantic feelings for the Fen, its history and its heritage. But the accusations of "Traitor" and "Judas" had cut through him like a knife. He realised that that was how it must seem, after he had so vociferously persuaded the town that it must fight for the Fen and all it meant to the community - that he had let them down badly, let Bungay down badly. They were unlikely to respect the fact that he felt he had done it for what he felt were the right and honourable reasons.

But even now he was not sure about himself and whether he had balanced things out properly in his mind.

What had he done?

Danny remained at home for the rest of the day, doing nothing, eating nothing, agonising over what had happened and what would happen now. The phone rang twice, but he didn't answer it. He tried to rationalise:

After all, his view, though it carried a lot of weight with the campaigners, was only one person's view, and was just one that the inspector would take into account in compiling his report and forming his recommendations to the Secretary of State at the Department of Food and Rural Affairs - though in reality, of course, he never saw such reports. Mr Watson was an experienced man who would weigh very carefully the argument on each side and would look at it from a planning point of view, objectively and unemotionally. In his time he would have heard many passionate pleas for or against planning applications, and was well able to keep them in proper perspective.

Eventually, around 6pm, he had a cup of coffee, put on his coat, called Megan, and made for the Fen in the early twilight. He needed fresh air, and so did Meg after another day on her own.

The dank, overcast mistiness of the morning had cleared and stars were now visible in breaks in the cloud as they took the familiar route over the bypass, through the kissing gate and down the central track that more or less separated the Hards from the Lows, past the now shadowy scrub oaks and more mature trees, through the curtain of silver birch and willows and into Iris Glade. Megan, as usual, was everywhere, back and forth, seeking out the smells and frequently returning to her master for re-assurance.

They reached the wooden bridge across the dyke, and Danny leant despondently on the rail, facing the town but looking down into the still, dark water beneath, and the tangle of nettles and reeds that reached wildly over from either side - a confused and random example of nature's patterns.

Danny stared at it, unmoving, for some time, his mind no more clear than the view beneath and no more clear than ten hours earlier in that same spot. He had made his decision spontaneously at the inquiry and must stick to it. He'd washed his hands of it - the inspector must now decide.

Eventually he straightened and looked towards the town, and the silhouettes of St Mary's Church, the factory and a few rooftops just visible, and Earsham's "pencil" church spire to the west. The trees were dark, just the outline of their trunks and heads, as you see in children's picture books. Over to the left across the grazing meadow the lights twinkled cosily form the windows of Vineyard House.

All was peace, solitude, calm - no sound, save the occasional quiet splash made by a fish or river creature.

But there was sound inside Danny's head - the sounds of "Traitor!" and "Judas!" echoed shrilly there, and would not go away, however much he tried to still them. Suddenly he was hated by Bungay, not admired, and soon the haven of the Fen would no longer be available - this Eden scene would explode into the hubbub and noise of a housing estate, shops, pubs and nightclubs and all they brought with them.

And now he had contributed to it, he was sure, by his words to the inspector.

Suddenly there was another noise, faint at first. Megan, sitting patiently as ever, pricked up her ears. It was the sound of feet brushing through the Fen grass. Danny strained his eyes through the early darkness, and soon made out the shape of a figure moving towards them. Who else could be about in the darkness?

"Danny...Danny, is that you? Oh, hello Megan - so it must be you."

"Jenny? What one earth are you doing here at this time of day, on your own. You're usually still at the office."

Jenny reached the bridge, and leaned on the rail beside Danny. Megan, who had run towards her to greet her, resumed her sitting position beside them, ears cocked.

"I came to find you. I rang you a couple of times and there was no answer."

"Oh, you wanted a quote from me. I'm sorry, Jenny, I should have realised..."

"No, the story's written. No, I...I was worried about you Danny. I could see how stressed you were this morning, how difficult it was for you, and then you left so quickly. I wished I could have offered you some support, knowing how deeply you feel about this place." Her voice was gentle, caring.

"Then when I couldn't get you at home, and when you weren't there when I called round a little while ago, I was more worried still. You seemed so confused. I thought you might…well…"

"Do something silly? No, I wouldn't do that, Jenny, never. You need never worry about that. At least…" Danny scowled. "…at least, not as silly as I did this morning."

Jenny caressed his arm, tenderly, comfortingly.

"Saying you'd changed your mind, you mean? Was it silly, Danny, do you think it was silly?"

Danny let out a long, heavy, audible sigh, that almost ended as a shout.

"I just don't know! You heard what I said, and how I tried to rationalise what I was saying. But I really don't know."

He shook his head and turned towards Jenny and put his hands on her shoulders.

"Was I saying the right thing at the right time? Or was I saying the wrong thing at the wrong time? Or the right thing at the wrong time….? It was just that, well - I suddenly felt selfish, I suppose, wanting the Fen, this place, for me…that the whole campaign was selfish when there really are lots of Yvonne Delgardos desperate for a home and there are no places to build them any more except green fields. I suppose I suddenly felt a NIMBY - one of the not in my back yard brigade - and I always said I would never be one of those."

He paused, and sighed again: "And now, saying that here, in the dark, it sounds so darn pious and righteous and I don't want that either…oh, it's such a mess!" He almost hissed the final word.

"Danny, Danny, don't," Jenny said soothingly putting her arms on his, too. "Don't agonise like this, don't castigate yourself. You did what you thought was right, and that took courage."

"Do you think it was right, Jen?" Danny looked earnestly into her eyes, which shone bright in the dark.

"Well now, I'm just an objective newspaper reporter -

that's not for me to say!" And her eyes twinkled bright too, and he smiled for the first time that day.

"And, by the way," she added in the same tone, " I think you were influenced by the pretty Yvonne in that decision! She reminded me of someone, did she you? Either that or I'd seen her somewhere before."

"The face was familiar - it was the face in the header above the stage. It was rather uncanny. Did you notice it?"

"Mmmm, maybe," said Jenny, doubtfully.

Danny paused, and added: "But no, her prettiness did not influence me - it was what she said, and she seemed so desolate, so pathetic, close to a breakdown almost. That did sway me - to what extent I don't know.

"Jenny -" the two were still clutching each others arms, close "- Jenny, thanks for everything, for caring, for being here at this moment - here in this special place. Thanks for finding me. I feel better now, even if my mind isn't any clearer. Thank you."

He added, almost in a whisper: "You know, if any woman could move me, it would be you, Jen."

She did not reply. There, in that dark haven so precious to both of them, deep in the embrace of God's territory, on that lonely wooden bridge in Iris Glade, the separate silhouettes of those two people gently became one as they enfolded and held each other, cosily close for some time.

Megan remained patient. And the barn owl, moving white in the darkness of her methodical search for food, looked down approvingly.

Their leisurely walk back, hand in hand, was one of those every couple will recall from their first days of romance - talking gently and quietly, the whispered feeling, the frequent stops for a close and loving embrace, the funny spontaneous remarks, the togetherness, the security of knowing you have someone to depend on, be with, and make plans with.

But the feelings were abruptly interrupted as Danny and Jenny reached the gate of his home and walked up the path.

The front window was smashed, the words "Traitor" and "Judas" daubed in red paint across the front door, by the light of the street light they could see plants and shrubs in the garden had been destroyed, and inside the front room there was glass everywhere, and beer bottles, some of which had been emptied across the carpet, lay broken too. A wooden placard with the Save our Fen slogan on it, rested upside down against a chair, where it had landed after being hurled through the window.

"What on earth....?"

Danny did not need to finish his low growl. Jenny gripped his arm.

"Oh no! The pigs! How could they? How could they do this to you? Do they think this is going to help their cause?"

Danny picked up the placard and hurled it back through where the window pane used to be, into the garden. He said nothing for a while - just walked among the debris of his front room.

Then he said: "It's anarchy. Commercial greed on one side, anarchy on the other. Can't people see a common middle way these days? People that do this sort of thing have no interest in the future of the common - it's just another excuse to jump on the bandwagon of opposition and violence."

He paused for several moments, then took a deep breath: "Oh well - I'll just have to clear this lot up and ring the glazier in the morning."

"I'll help you, Dan - it won't take long if we do it together."

"No, you go home Jen - it's late. I'll sort it out. I'll ring you tomorrow."

He insisted despite her protestations. They hugged tightly and long, and looked into each others eyes before Jenny left reluctantly, turning to blow a kiss from the gate as she disappeared. Danny put Megan into the kitchen and shut the door to make sure she did not get glass in her paws, and began to clear up.

"This will change nothing," he told himself firmly.

The next edition of the Gazette carried the story of the attack, with a picture of Danny in his devastated garden. Jenny had written it, and Danny had given her some quotes, restrained and considered, and saying his stance remained the same on the issue - he was withdrawing his opposition to the housing plan.

There were comments from Fenton condemning the attack and praising Danny's integrity in his change of heart, and from the Town Reeve. George Bell also offered sympathy, condemned what he called "the loutish animals" responsible for the attack, but concentrated mainly on his gratitude to Danny for ending his opposition to the scheme.

The police, meanwhile, were reported to be actively pursuing the matter and issued an appeal for information from anyone who may have seen anything or anyone suspicious near Danny's home during the evening.

Meanwhile, the inquiry over, the inspector went back to London to begin the task of compiling what would clearly be a lengthy report on what he had heard and to draw up his recommendations. It was expected to be months before the recommendation, and the decision from that by the Secretary of State, was known, and so it proved. Outney Fen went through its changing wardrobe - the grey of late autumn, the white of winter snow and ice, and the emerging brighter colours of spring, the fresh green buds turning to young leaves, the carpet of snowdrops on the spot where once stood George Baldry's house just on the Norfolk side of the river, the firs flag irises in the dykes; before taking on the brilliant gold mantle of the gorse in full bloom on the Hards and the softer yellow of buttercups and then the generous splashes of purple loosestrife and willow herb as summer blossomed fully again.

Through that time of nature's sleeping and waking Danny and Jenny spent more and more time together, talking, debating, planning, agonising, and loving, either at Danny's home, quickly returned to normal following the attack, or Jenny's Beccles flat. It was a loving and a merging of spirits and souls nurtured by regular walks on the Fen with Megan, and the comfort that gave them as they awaited the decision which would have such an impact on many lives. The quietness and beauty of those acres moved them together as they wandered, hand in hand or arm in arm, at dawn or at sunset, feeling its security and each other's love.

But despite their closeness, their views on one issue remained opposed - Danny was steadfast in believing that his own views on protecting the Fen should take second place to the vital needs of people like Yvonne Delgardo which the housing scheme would provide for. And if he wavered in that, his views were re-inforced again each time they were at the Fisher Theatre - where he and Jenny frequently enjoyed productions and films, as well as its restaurant - and his eyes encountered the face on the proscenium header.

Jenny remained convinced that the opposition to the scheme should continue - that the housing needs could easily be provided elsewhere, in other ways, without destroying Bungay's greatest asset that Outney represented. They debated the issue frequently as the weeks and months went by. Danny had difficulty in fully explaining his change of heart, except to say that he felt it was a matter of priorities and that the dire needs of those seeking homes must be considered before the romantic, environmental and historic views of those fortunate enough to have good homes, important though those views were. And it was only his view - the view of one person among the many continuing to campaign vigorously against the scheme.

Jenny felt sure, in the early stages of their love, that their walks on the Fen would help him realise that it should not be lost to the arrogant cause of out and out commercialism.

Certainly as time went on and Bungay people continued their campaign against the scheme, Danny became more edgy. He had become almost an outcast with many people, and the accusations of traitor and Judas hurt him considerably, much more than he showed outwardly. His house or car were not targeted again, but verbal attacks continued, even from people he knew well - others were simply distant and terse when they met him in the street, or collected their children from school.

It was unpleasant, but his response was to withdraw, spend less time out in the town, but more time on the Fen, with Jenny and Megan, or on his own. He spent more time there than ever before, as if needing to drink on its reviving and sustaining elixir before the source of that potion disappeared for ever.

The issue continued to be covered and debated in the media as the months went by. The letters columns were full of the work of people wanting to express outspoken views, mainly against the development plan but there was the occasional maverick spirit offering it support. The protesters organised a march through the town, supported by hundreds of people, and held a sit-in on the Fen for two days, until a prolonged week of rain dispersed them.

Pilgrim Homes remained confident that the decision would go their way. Surveyors and other staff were regularly seen on the Fen, taking readings and assessing levels in preparation for starting work - they made it clear that if the decision went their way the bulldozers would move in without delay to begin the task of providing "much needed affordable homes for many needy people, and splendid facilities for the community of Bungay to enjoy."

They said it would be the biggest scheme in the country so far in response to the Government's call for house-building to accelerate.

CHAPTER ELEVEN

PILGRIM'S confidence proved well founded. It was July again when the inspector's recommendation, inevitably rubber-stamped by the Secretary of State, was made public. It fully outlined the arguments on both sides as he had seen it, paid tribute to both the developers and the "compelling views of those who campaigned against the loss of the wonderful natural amenity that Outney Fen represents," and made clear that the developers had to adhere to the stringent planning requirements attached to the scheme, but concluded:

"This has been a difficult inquiry to assess because it is in many ways a pioneering project which will undoubtedly have far reaching affects on Bungay as a town and a community. It is something of a test case, and therefore one likely to be repeated in many communities throughout the country where green sites are being looked at to meet the housing need. There never has been any dispute that that critical housing need exists.

"I have taken every view into account, but on planning grounds and under the Government's current guidelines on housing targets and how they should be achieved, my recommendation is that permission for this planning application should be confirmed.

"I am writing to the relevant planning authorities to underline the need for all provisos and Section 106 agreements in the approval to be strictly adhered to, and for their building control departments to see every aspect of the design is followed in detail.

"In coming to my recommendations I have taken the view that, on balance, Bungay as a community will have benefits from the scheme which in time will outweigh the loss of Outney Fen as it is at the moment. It is particularly important that the scheme should help many young families desperate for a home they can afford."

Jenny received the advanced press release at the Gazette office on a Monday morning - another blazing shimmering, high summer July day. It was too late to contact Danny before he left for school, and she had to wait till lunch-time to get hold of him, to break the news.

"Danny, we've got the inspector's report. The appeal has been dismissed. The scheme is going ahead. It's going to happen."

Her voice was breaking, full of emotion. Danny tried to soothe her, and asked exactly what the report had said. She read him the relevant sentences.

"Danny, I don't know if I can write this story. I've got too close to it, too involved. I don't know if I'm able to write a balanced report any more."

"Yes you can - you're a professional. You've written lots of stories before when you haven't agreed with people's views on them or the effect they may have on people. Try to look upon it as just another story. I'll help you."

"Danny! What do *you* feel, now that it's actually going to happen? This is a wake up call! It's not a possibility any more, it's real. That Fen means everything to you."

"Yes to me - one person. One person who has a good job, a comfortable home, a contented life. The Fen is somewhere I can go to relax and enjoy the peace, the spirituality, the inspiration it provides. But is that enough to deny many other people the chance of a good home in a largely rural location, and it is enough to deny other Bungay people the amenities the town needs? I'll find other places that provide spirituality and peace and inspiration. I was content to let the inquiry make the decision on the Fen - it would have been great if it could be kept as it is, but that's a selfish view."

"Danny, who are you - Pontius Pilate? You're washing your hands of something you believe fervently is right because you are afraid to go with your convictions.

You're not being true to yourself! You're not the person I knew any more. Where's your spine? I don't...I...I'm going. I can't go on with this anymore."

"Jenny, Jenny..." Danny tried to soothe her. "I know you're upset. But no one really wins in things like this. It is all about compromises..."

"Compromises? Where is the compromise now? Pilgrim's haven't compromised - it's a winner takes all situation and they've won, haven't they? And you haven't compromised - you've capitulated, to salve your conscience. If the appeal had been upheld you'd have been able to say you had tried to be objective in your view. Now the plan is going ahead you can say you think that is for the best. You've washed your hands of any decision. Pontius Pilate! How pathetic!"

Danny was taken aback by Jenny's uncharacteristic venom, and his silence allowed her to continue:

"I don't think this is about the Fen at all - I think it is about you and your conscience and wanting to be seen as a good, caring person. Well that's not how you come across to me, Danny boy, you seem to me to be someone who can't carry their convictions through when the going gets tough. I don't like what I see and hear at all. The Fen is going to go and so its our friendship!"

Jenny was in tears as she put the phone down and put her hands to her face. Danny was startled at the re-action, but had no time to dwell on it - he had a class of energetic eight-year-olds to try to control on a hot, energy sapping afternoon. There was no opportunity to get his head round Jenny's feelings and what she was saying. He knew her stance on the issue and respected it, but she had always remained calm, until now.

She had always loved the Fen in the same way that many people did, but not, until now, with the same passion, outwardly, that he had always had.

It was early evening before he was able to get away and make for the Fen again. It was still hot, the sun beating down from a blue sky, the skylarks soaring, people in shorts and T-shirts walking their dogs, golfers enjoying an evening game over to the left as he made his way down the main track between the Hards and the Lows, scenting the aromas of the sun on the gorse and the heathery grass and the reedy dykes.

It was just as it was that day - was it only two years ago? - when he had got back from the common late in the evening to find out about the plans to sell it for housing. It had seemed just a fantasy, but had led to a confusion of feelings and re-actions as it became reality through a series of meetings, and the inquiry. For Danny it had brought the realisation that sometimes sacrifices had to be made for the benefit of those in real need if the demand merited it.

And it had brought him love with Jenny - a relationship that had developed almost because of the Fen controversy and the battle to save it, a fight he had now conceded for the sake of those in dire need of homes and the chance to make a life for themselves.

But what was Jenny feeling now, Danny wondered, as he moved toward Iris Glade, through the cool high grass and the scrub oaks and the willowherb and blackberry bushes and hawthorn that had for so long been part of his Eden. Had she filed a story on the inquiry result, or had she been too upset to do so? Had her feelings for him changed so suddenly in the emotion of realising that this beautiful, atmospheric piece of God's earth was to be lost for ever to the bricks and concrete of homes and other community facilities?

His mind was confused and his heart was heavy as he moved through the curtain of trees that was Iris Glade to the magical meadow beyond, beside the deep dyke and towards the river at the bottom of the Common - that area inspirational in its atmosphere, where he was close to God, and nature, and the peace that both brought to the scene.

Jenny was standing on the bridge. Danny had intended to call on her after visiting the common to get his thoughts together, but now he realised he had half expected her to be there.

Her presence somehow enhanced the spot as she leant on the rail, looking into the dyke as he had done so often himself, her silky brown hair falling forward over her loose top which revealed a bare midriff above her white shorts. But she looked a forlorn and lonely figure, there beside the deep dyke and the grazing meadow with the cattle statues, under the backdrop of the Vineyard Hills.

Danny was almost at the bridge before Jenny looked up and saw him there. She smiled a weak smile, and slowly straightened up. Danny moved close to her and gently put his arms round her and cradled her head in his shoulder.

"How are you feeling?" he whispered.

"Drained." She hesitated and went on:

"I still can't understand your feelings. But I suppose you must still love this place as you are here."

The remark seemed to carry a barb.

"Oh, Jenny - you know I'll always love this place and what it means to me, and to us..."

"Well you'd better make the most of it because it won't be here very much longer, will it!"

Jenny pulled away from him moodily and stood by the stile at the side of the bridge.

"Danny, do you take in the reality of this situation? This Fen, Iris Glade, the owls and herons and gorse and beauty and peace and God's presence you say you feel so strongly - none of those will be here any more. But you're not prepared to fight for it. I can't understand it."

Danny heaved a heavy sigh.

"I'm not sure I do, Jen. I just feel I should think about what other people need..."

"That's an excuse for not making up your mind and having the courage of your convictions," Jenny almost snapped at him, her back still towards him and still facing the gently flowing cool waters of the Waveney.

"There are always two sides to any debate, often both

compelling - you have to make up your mind which is best for you as you see the wider picture, and then stick to it, not prevaricate!"

"Well I have decided and I am sticking to it. That's what I told the inspector. I changed my mind after hearing what Yvonne Delgardo had to say. I though that was a more compelling argument than mine, however strongly I felt about it."

Danny was talking firmly now.

"Then we will continue to take a different viewpoint on this. I'll continue to report it fairly and evenly as a professional journalist, but in my own time I will fight against it right up to the time the bulldozers move in - and beyond that. I'm not giving up on what I believe in, even if you do - Pontius Pilate."

The last phrase was almost spat out, as a disparaging sneer, as Jenny climbed the stile, jumped down the other side and made off briskly along the banks of the Waveney towards Vineyard House.

Danny hesitated, heaved another heavy sigh, and followed her.

"Jenny," he called. "Jenny. We know each others views on this - we been over it a hundred times. We all have to live with our convictions. I want to see this beautiful place, this paradise, retained as much as anyone else, but I can't insist on that when there are so many people like Yvonne Delgardo so desperate for homes that they cannot get in any other way. I'm not backing Pilgrim's scheme - I'm just not fighting against it any more."

"You're so right Danny - so right! You're just not fighting full stop. You haven't got any fight in you when it comes to it, have you? You run away from what you really believe in. I can't understand you any more. I really believed in you and admired you, but now…."

Jenny suddenly stopped and turned to face Danny as he moved towards her. She paused, and when she continued there was almost a pleading in her voice.

"Danny, Danny - don't you remember Mrs Baldwin's

words at the inquiry all those months ago as she pleaded with the inspector? Don't you remember her passion, her anguish, her belief in what she was saying about that place that surrounds us now? She will never change her mind about it, she won't give up, and nor will I. And yet who was first to go to Yvonne Delgardo when she broke down? Yes, Mrs Baldwin. She felt for her, empathised with her, completely understood her, comforted her - but that did not make her waver from her own convictions. Look around you now, Danny - look at this pasture, look at the gorse over there, the curtain of trees, the Vineyard Hills, the river, Bath House. And look - over there…there's our barn owl.

"Can you tell me you are not prepared to fight for this, whatever the cost? Well I am - and there are still others who will. Maybe you're just too soft - you're certainly too soft for me…No, don't follow me…" as she turned and walked off again she put her hand up.

"… I'm going home on my own. I need time to think about a lot of things. And us."

Danny hesitated, made to follow Jenny as she walked off, then stopped, and shrugged. Better to let her go, he thought.

He stood and watched her slim figure, arms folded and head down, as she made her way along the riverbank, past the lone willow tree, past the Vineyard House, now in shadow on the opposite side of the river, and along to the next stile. She climbed it slowly, without looking back, and continued to make her way through the pasture, beside the cattle still grazing.

Megan sat, puzzled, by his side, after at first beginning to follow Jenny. Now, as Danny eventually turned back towards the bridge, she dutifully followed him.

Again he stood, leaning on the rail with his back to the river, facing the Fen and the town on the horizon. It was getting towards dusk, and he could just make out the silhouette of St Mary's Church through the trees, beyond the stark shape of Clay's book printing factory.

All around him was still, save the occasional plop-plop from a fish surfacing in the river, the sound of the grasshoppers, and the barn owl still doing his systematic evening search no more than 30 yards from where he stood.

There he remained for some time, gazing into the dyke, or straightening and surveying the Fen scene he knew so well but which still filled him with contentment, peace, and spiritual well-being. He tried to gather his thoughts on how Jenny was feeling, what she had said, whether she was right, whether he should change his mind and take up the fight for the Fen and Iris Glade again, even at this late stage.

But Danny could not concentrate, could not organise his thoughts, could not focus on the issues and how he really felt about everything.

One thing he did know however - how much he loved this place, its tranquillity, its unchallenging friendship, its way of enfolding and protecting those who walked there and gave themselves to its sanctuary.

How long he remained there he was not sure. But when eventually, to Megan's relief, he moved off and made his way through Iris Glade, it was virtually dark, with just a glimmer of light from the sun which had disappeared behind the Vineyard Hills, and the imperceptible sound of nature preparing to sleep.

It was almost dark as, two or three minutes later, they moved through the silver birch and brambles and hawthorns of Iris Glade. Megan suddenly stopped and pricked up her ears, looking through the trees.

"Hello – Peter?"

The shadow of a man approached through the twilight. His voice was gentle, and he had a staff in his hand. Almost immediately, he added:

"I'm sorry – I thought you were someone else. Forgive me."

His piercing, compassionate eyes met Danny's and held them, unflinching, for what seemed many seconds before he finally said; "G'night," and walked off towards the river, quickly lost in the darkness.

Danny watched him go for a few seconds, before turning homewards again. He knew most people who walked regularly on the Fen, particularly at that time, but it was a face he had never seen before.

As he walked back towards the silhouette of the town, the words repeated themselves in his head:

"Hello- Peter?"

Why had he thought he was Peter? Who was Peter? Who was the bearded man who had spoken his name?

Danny's mind was troubled and confused. But as he entered the town and glanced back to the darkness of the Fen he once more had that sense of reality, as if he had left a dream behind, and the old man was merely a spectre from that dream.

"Jenny?"

It was three days later, and Danny had decided to contact her to see how she was.

"Jenny, how are things? I've missed you."

"Hi Danny. I know, I know I've missed you too. I'm sorry I went off like that but...well, it's just how I felt...how I feel. It hasn't changed."

"I understand that, Jen. This is such an awful business. But I hope one day you'll come to respect my view, however much you oppose it."

"Maybe," said Jenny, doubtfully.

"Can we meet?"

"We'll, things are pretty hectic at the moment - you'll have seen that in the national press as well as the Gazette. Everyone is focussing on this issue, locally, regionally and nationally. The feeling is that if the Government can make a decision like this at Bungay it can happen to similar green sites anywhere in the country. I'm doing little else but stories on it at the moment - and when I do get time I'm trying to see what the action group can do to make a stand even at this eleventh hour. You'll have heard that the date for the start of work is July 16th?"

"Yes, I know. It's the date I'm taking my class to London to see a production of A Midsummer Night's Dream by the Royal Shakespeare Company. I won't be able to be there, unfortunately."

"Would you have been there anyway?" said Jenny laconically. "Just to watch the start of the desecration."

"I'm not sure I could be there to see that happen. From what I've read it could be a pretty grim occasion, with some pretty aggressive people planning a final protest."

"It could be nasty," Jenny agreed. "But you can't blame them for having a go. A lot of people feel very strongly and very passionately that the Fen should be left as it is and will fight it to the very end."

Danny sensed another barb.

"Look, I've got to go," Jenny said. "Work to do. Have a good trip to London."

CHAPTER THIRTEEN

THE coach trip to London was noisy, but reasonably orderly. The weather had cooled, and was overcast and breezy so the confines of the coach were not as stuffy as they might have been. Children on an outing were always excited, and more so as they were also looking forward to the summer holidays in a couple of weeks' time.

Summer holidays - how would they be spending them, Danny thought as he watched the countryside go by. When he was that age he and his mates spent most of the time on the Fen - fishing, swimming in the river, looking for birds nests, walking the dog, making dens in the gorse and picnicking in them. Today's children would probably be on holidays abroad, or watching videos, playing on their Play Stations or going to discos - enjoying the open spaces around them would not be part of their holiday itinerary.

And it dawned on Danny that even if they wanted to, they would no longer be able to revel in the activities provided by Outney Fen. That option was about to be lost for ever. He felt a sharp stab of depression in his stomach at that realisation.

The Shakespeare production was at the Lyceum Theatre in the West End. The 50 children tumbled out of the coach and into the theatre foyer in a more or less orderly way, bags over their shoulders or under their arms. They would probably not appreciate the skill and nuances of the great bard's pen, but it would serve as an introduction, and something they would remember when the time came for them to study his works in more detail, Danny thought.

They were certainly in awe when the curtain went up on the first act and they saw the lavishness of the scenery and the costumes. The comedy came over well from the experienced cast, many of them household names and seen in top films and on television. The children recognised them and whispered loudly to each other as they did so. Danny had to signal to them to be quiet.

Most he recognised himself. Others were less familiar, and the minor parts were taken by those hoping to make their mark eventually in the acting world.

It was halfway through the first half when Queen Titania's handmaidens came on to the stage, pretty and gossamer-like in costume and make-up. And as he surveyed their faces, one struck Danny as particularly familiar.

Where had he seen that face before? Striking features, rather sad eyes, a tolerant mouth.

He searched his memory throughout the scene, and kept glimpsing her. Of course - the programme would have her name. He found the page: "Hand maidens - Natasha Murphy, Gabriella Collingwood, Petra Brealey, Siobhan Driscoll."

None rang any bells at all. Amidst the projected dialogue and the frequent laughter Danny wracked his brains to bring to mind that face and where he had seen it before. Where oh, where was it - it must have been in some play or a film he had seen somewhere before? It would nag away at him till he recalled it - he would probably wake up in the middle of the night and it would be there.

Which theatres had he been to? The Fisher Theatre of course, and a couple of months ago the Theatre Royal in Norwich, and…

"The Fisher Theatre…the face in the proscenium header!"

It suddenly struck him. And a split second later:

"Yvonne Delgardo! That's Yvonne Delgardo!"

Danny almost blurted it out loud as the realisation dawned on him. And as his memory suddenly came freely, he remembered that she had featured in a television series two years ago which had become a classic of its type. She had had a small role, but a key one. That is why she had been so familiar when he had seen her in the witness box at the inquiry at the theatre. Yes, the face in the header was like her, but it was that television role that he had remembered her for.

Yet at the inquiry she had mentioned nothing about being an actress - simply a single parent desperately in need of a home to call her own. And she wasn't mentioned in the programme, although she could have a stage name, Danny thought.

The whole thing puzzled him, and during the interval he left his colleagues to keep control of the children as they bought their ice-creams and drinks and popcorn, and sought out someone connected with the production.

He was lucky - the assistant producer was just coming out of the staff door.

"Can you help me?" Danny asked. "Sorry to hold you up, but I've brought a school party from Suffolk to see the play, and I noticed that one of the cast comes from our area - from Beccles I believe. I just thought it would make a good follow-up for them if she could come into school one day to talk about her acting career."

"Beccles? Never heard of it," said the assistant manager brusquely. "Who is it you're asking about?"

"Well, I believe her name is Yvonne Delgardo, but I guess she has a stage name - she is one of the handmaidens."

"I doubt she'd have a stage name - that largely went out of fashion years ago."

Danny described the actress to him, and the assistant manager lightened immediately.

"Ah, that's Gabby - Gabriella Collingwood. She's a great actress, with a great future. But she's certainly not from...where did you say?...Beccles? Suffolk? I know for a fact she's never lived in Suffolk. She's from Wiltshire, actually. Now she lives with Bob Hargreaves, the lighting manager. When she is not in productions like this she does a lot of one off engagements, and I bet she commands a good fee too, judging by the place they live in in Hampstead."

"Has she never lived in Beccles then?"

"No, not to my knowledge, and I've known Gabby most of her life - her parents were in the theatre businesses you see, and I more or less saw her grow up. Great little actress - you must have seen her on television."

"Yes…yes, I have."

Danny hardly heard what he had said. He thanked him and apologised for interrupting, and returned to his charges, who were beginning to move back into the auditorium for the second half of A Midsummer Night's Dream.

Through the following hour he was hardly aware of the dramatic production in front of him - he could think of little else than of Yvonne Delgardo, and the more he went over it in his mind the more indignant he became.

So she was not a real person - it had all been an act, skilfully carried out by Gabriella Collingwood. There was no Yvonne, with children who were cooped up in her mother's home in cramped conditions, and no alcoholics coming in to see her mother at regular intervals. It was a story which had been fabricated solely to affect the course of the inquiry and to win permission for the Iris Glade development.

And another thing occurred to Danny - clearly Gabriella had been paid to do the job, and if that was the case it must have been Pilgrim Homes who had paid her, or at least George Bell privately. It was all a sham - the inspector had been conned into thinking she was desperate for a house thanks to a scripted story skilfully delivered by a convincing actress.

"Yes and it conned me too - to such an extent that I was prepared to give up my Fen to help people like her," Danny thought to himself. "And she's come between me and Jenny. And I've realised too late how stupid I've been! What a mess! What a mess!"

He put his head in his hands in despair, oblivious of the laughter and re-action to the activity on stage. He remained like that for some seconds, and the pupil sitting next to him said in a wavering voice:

"Are you all right, Mr Tegerdine?"

"Yes Chloe, yes thanks. Just a bit…a bit tired. Are you enjoying the play?"

Danny himself was scarcely aware of what stage the play was at - he could only think of how he had betrayed all those who got behind the Save Our Fen campaign that he had instigated. Yes, they were right to brand him a traitor, he had let them down badly in pulling out so abruptly because of the made up story featuring the fictional Yvonne Delgardo.

"At least I can let Jenny know what I've discovered - I'm sure there must be a story in it for her even if it is to late to stop the project," Danny thought to himself. And the searing pain in his stomach hit him again as he realised that at that very moment the bulldozers and earth removers would have begun the task of obliterating the land that had served Bungay so well for so many centuries.

But when he tried to contact Jenny as soon as the show was over, at about 5.15pm, there was no reply, just Jenny's answer phone with the usual request to leave a message. He declined it.

By the time the coach arrived back at the school in Bungay, after a stop for a meal, and a second emergency stop for a visit to the toilet by one of the children, and after he had stayed until the last child had been collected by their parents, Danny made for home. It was too late to try Jenny again, and he could not bring himself to take Megan down to the Fen to see the deep scars to its surface that would have already been made there. He took her for a quick walk to the Castle Hills so she could stretch her legs after being at home alone all day.

He slept fitfully, restlessly during a humid night, the events of the day going over and over in his mind. Overriding it was the guilt he felt at letting down his town, his friends, the people of Bungay in general, in giving up the fight for the Fen at a time when the campaign was reaching a climax. Now the fight was lost, the Fen would be lost and he had probably lost Jenny too.

"What have I done?" he kept repeating to himself as he lay tossing and turning in the darkness.

CHAPTER FOURTEEN

HE FINALLY slept towards dawn, and was awoken by the dawn chorus - the beautiful sounds of the robins, blackbirds, thrushes, sparrows, tits and starlings, discordant but somehow harmonising into a melody of nature. Danny looked at the clock - it was just after 5am, yet is still seemed fairly dark, and when he looked out of the window he saw why. There were heavy low clouds and it was rainy steadily. The garden looked saturated and there were puddles along the path. It was a gloomy, depressing morning for July and it reflected Danny mood.

It was no good trying to sleep again. He got up, went downstairs and put the kettle on for a cup of coffee. As he waited for it to boil he realised he had not checked his answerphone when he got in, and he switched it on. There was one new message:

"Hi Danny, its Jenny. Not sure when you'll get this message, but I thought you'd want to know the start of the work on the Fen has been delayed for 24 hours. They're going to start early tomorrow, about six I think. Wasn't sure if you wanted to be there. See you sometime."

Danny, suddenly wide awake, switched it off. So the project had not started - there was still time to make a last protest. Still time, if belatedly, to re-affirm his opposition to what was to happen. It might be too late to make any difference, too late to prevent the Fen being mutilated, but not too late to join the final display of feelings at what was happening.

He paused as he poured water into his coffee cup. His presence wouldn't go down very well with those who had continued the campaign without him - they would see it as too lame and too late. Indeed they would probably see it as a hollow gesture proffered because he knew it was too late. Perhaps it would be best to stay away.

Danny sat down at the kitchen table and looked into his coffee cup for sometime, deep in thought, Megan as always sitting with eyes fixed on him. Then he got up suddenly.

"No!" he said out loud, causing Megan to bark. "George Bell is bound to be there - at least I can ask him in public why he deliberately deceived the inspector at the public inquiry and conned everyone else. And Jenny will be there - she'd be interested in it from a news point of view. No - I'm going down there."

It was 5.15am. He hurriedly made himself some toast and marmalade, ate it quickly and washed it down with his coffee, gave Megan a couple of biscuits to keep her happy, and prepared to go.

It was still pouring with rain, harder than earlier, Danny thought, as he looked out of the window at the leaden clouds which seemed unbroken across that unseasonal July sky. He put on a coat over his shirt, but there was no point in taking an umbrella in that rain - it would be next to useless.

He was soaked almost before he reached the end of Quaves Lane and turned into St Mary's Street - so was Megan, trotting by his side. They splashed along the pavement as water rushed down the gutter beside them. At the problem spots in the town in such weather, particularly outside St Edmund's Church and in front of the Swan Inn, large lakes of water had formed and water spilt over the gutters of the shops along the streets.

As he walked briskly through the town, Danny wondered what it would be like on the common - pretty squelchy, probably, with the rain soaking into the paths made hard by the long spell of dry, hot weather which had preceded this deluge.

Surprisingly it seemed to him, there were other people moving through the town in the same direction, undeterred by the rain, some of them carrying protest placards, protected from the rain by hastily attached clear plastic covers. They had obviously heard that there would be an early start to the work, Danny thought.

But he was not prepared for the scene that greeted him as he crossed the bypass and moved through the main gate on to the Fen - open wide, on this occasion, presumably to give access to the earthmovers.

They were visible in the middle distance, but they were surrounded by at least 500 people, waving placards and banners and chanting, as more moved on to the Fen from all directions. Lines of police officers were there, with at least half a dozen mounted police, their riders wearing long blue police mackintoshs, and crash helmets with the black and white check band of the police livery around them.

The nearer he got, the more noisy it became. It was a sinister scene, with a lot of shouting, and Danny realised that many in the crowd were in an aggressive mood, pointing at the police, and at three people standing on the back of a construction truck. Close to them was a semi-circle of press photographers, television cameras and radio microphones, to record the ceremony and the scene which would mark the beginning of the end of a facility that had been used by local people for a millennium.

On all of them, the rain poured down. The huge wheels of the earthmovers had already made dark scars in the ground, and the trampling of the crowds breaking up the soft surface was having its affect too, so that over an area of a couple of hundred square yards around the spot chosen for the first digging the ground already resembled a quagmire.

It was a grey, gloomy, dismal panorama, so different to the mantle the peaceful common usually donned in high summer. The Vineyard Hills were barely visible in the background through the rain and the cloud which seemed to be enveloping the heights of them, so low was the weather's shroud lying over this scene, the symbolic death of one of nature's most beautiful settings. As Danny surveyed it as he got closer it seemed that the elements prevailing there were God's way of showing disapproval of the whole concept, and the loss of the Fen and Iris Glade to the local people.

He made his way to the press contingent to seek out Jenny. There she was - and as he caught sight of her, in her long, dark brown rain coat and round waterproof hat that had proved unable to prevent her dark hair becoming bedraggled and sticking to her cheeks, he thought how wonderfully pretty she was even in those conditions, and how stupid he had been to lose her through his misguided thinking and his betraying the Fen cause through forsaking his convictions.

"Hi Jenny!" he had to shout through the hubbub of the crowds and the sound of the rain.

She turned from the crowd she was with, and gave him a smile.

"Hello Danny - you got my message then?"

"Yes, about half an hour ago! Thanks for taking the trouble to phone - I wouldn't have known about the postponement otherwise."

"Well, I wasn't sure that you'd be interested."

She shrugged, and started to turn away, but he held her arm and drew her aside to a slightly less noisy spot.

"Jenny - I'm sorry, so sorry. I've been pretty stupid, I've been thinking along the wrong channels, and I've let everyone down..."

"It's a bit late to realise that now, Danny - what changed your mind?"

"The fact that I now know I was conned and that everyone has been conned by the Pilgrim bandwagon. And the inspector at the inquiry was conned too, by an impressive piece of acting."

"What on earth do you mean?"

Jenny put on a puzzled look, and dropped the off hand air she had adopted till then.

Danny recounted to her his visit to the West End and the woman he had seen on stage - who at the inquiry had been Yvonne Delgardo, but who in fact was a professional actress who had never had any connection with Beccles and had no children, either.

"And Pilgrim's must have known that - they must have recruited her to act the part to boost their planning application," he said as the rain continued to soak them and run down both their faces.

"Are you absolutely sure about this?" Jenny asked.

"As sure as I can be - it came from someone who knew her and her current partner well - they live in Hertfordshire. They know virtually nothing about Beccles. Look Jenny, I was conned and I shouldn't have been. But I'm back right behind the campaign now."

"It's a bit late for that now. But I don't need to tell you that. Work starts today. But if you are prepared to be quoted, and, better still if I can find someone from the production you saw who would talk to me about her, we can do a story in the Gazette that would seriously damage Pilgrim's reputation."

"It will make people even more angry at what's happening, but it's too late to stop the project. You can only do that by overturning the inquiry decision, and I'm not sure that's ever been done before."

"I know, I know. I'm sorry it took something like that to come to my senses. Looking back I don't know how it influenced me as much as it did in the first place. But that's me I suppose."

"Yes, I guess it is Danny. Perhaps I should say Pontius Pilate. Look, things are about to happen, and I'll need to get back to the office as soon as I can afterwards. Give me a ring later today and we'll talk more about it. May be we could have a up of coffee?"

"Yes, great idea. I'll do that."

Jenny turned to go, but on an impulse turned back and gave Danny a tender kiss on the cheek, and her brown eyes and genuine smile held his for an instant.

Then her brightness was gone, into the rain and into the crowds which were pushing through the mud and the wet closer to the truck from where the speeches would be made, undeterred by the weather. It was like the bright orange and turquoise flash of a kingfisher which darts close to the surface of the river before disappearing as quickly as it beauty is glimpsed.

Danny watched Jenny's slim figure until she was out of sight…

Still the rain lashed down, blown occasionally by a gusty breeze, but Pilgrim's were determined that the ceremony signalling the start of their project should go ahead as planned - clearly they just wanted to get it over and get on with the job. They had fixed the early starting time in the hope of avoiding large crowds and the publicity, but that clearly had not worked, Danny observed to himself. As he looked round at the scene, he estimated there must be 700-800 people there, despite the weather, with many carrying placards and some having bells and rattles to add to the noise and hubbub as the crowds moved towards the truck.

The mounted police formed a line in an effort to keep the crowds at a reasonable distance from the truck, the well trained horses moving sideways or forwards at the behest of their charges, fretting slightly, but under control, seemingly undeterred by the growing volume of sound that now included chants, "Pilgrims Out! Pilgrims Out! Pilgrims out!" and "Off our Land! Off, off, off our Land!"

George Bell was standing on the back of the truck, along with the Mayor, who was to perform the ceremony, and a third man, armed with a loud hailer, who finally attempted to bring the crowds to order.

Gradually the noise subsided, and the introductions could be heard, before the loud hailer was handed over to George Bell, like everyone else soaked to the skin but determined to get the event out of the way so work could start.

Danny could only catch snatches of what he said as many in the crowd attempted to drown him out with booing and renewed chants.

".....making a dream come true for the people of Bungay...bold decision by the planners...the town will come to see this scheme as the making of Bungay...this is an investment for you..."

It was the expected speech which few were able to fully take in. At the end, he handed over the loud hailer to the Mayor, his scarlet robe looking bedraggled and rain running off his chain of office. He attempted to tell the crowds that the council understood their concerns over the scheme but they were convinced that it would prove one of Bungay's greatest assets in years to come.

He was a man of few words - he took less than a minute, before George Bell led him down from the truck and into the cab of a digger which had been made ready for him to dig the first turf to signal the start of Iris Glade, and the end of a thousand years of grazing pasture.

The noise of the crowds and the chanting was renewed as he climbed into the cab beside the digger operator, and it rose to a crescendo as he pulled the levers which made the business end of the digger scoop into the sodden turf and make the first scar beside the blackberry bushes and willowherb and the gorse where generations of children had played and made camps.

Some applause could just be heard as he did so, but it was drowned out by the feelings of the majority who were still pushing forward towards the mounted police and the media gallery as television and press cameras tried to get the best of the pictures of the rain soaked scene.

Suddenly there was a new sound, a loud roar, almost a harmonious snarl of voices. For the first time Danny, standing some yards to the side of the digger, was aware of what appeared to be a mob of dark clad people, woollen hats pulled low over the heads, some with scarves round their faces.

And they were on the move at the back of the crowds, charging at a run, hurling sticks, stones and cans. Some were armed with staves as they pushed into the back of the main crowd, forcing it forward with their impetus and gutteral sounds.

There was little the crowd could do. They were impelled forward by the surge, towards the mounted police and towards the truck and digger and the gallery of cameramen and reporters, unable to get out of the way or turn back. Their chants and jeers turned to urgent cries and some screams as they were carried forward, unable to control their movement. Some stumbled, clawing at those next to them to save themselves as the dark mob continued their relentless forward momentum towards George Bell and the Mayor.

From where he stood Danny could only watch in horror. And suddenly he saw a missile hurtle towards one of the mounted police and strike his mount a vicious blow by the eye. The animal, despite its training, instinctively reared and bucked as it let out a cry of pain, its rear legs slipped from underneath it and it fell and rolled towards the crowd. One camera flew into the air as panic overtook the scene, anguished screams and shouts mingled with the chants of the mob as the horse fell and rolled and bucked, and people being impelled forward were pushed against it and its flailing legs as its rider was thrown on to the crowds.

In the mud and the rain, terrified people were scrambling to pick themselves up and get out of the way of the mass of bodies, still screaming, panic stricken. Those that could got out of the way and ran for safety. The felled horse managed to get back on its feet, blood coming from a nasty cut on its head, and bolted towards the bottom of the Fen.

Even the mob - some, Danny noticed, having Green Land Protection Unit daubed in paint on their clothing - finally realised something had gone wrong and held back.

It was a surreal, desolate scene of mud and grass, people lying stunned on the ground, the remaining mounted police trying to restore order. One man had blood pouring from a head wound, the teeming rain spreading the blood over his face and clothes; a woman clutched her shoulder, crying in pain, others nursed bruises and some were able to limp away as the crowds gradually cleared.

Danny, stunned, moved toward a small concerned group which had gathered round one person still lying on the ground, another kneeling beside it, and others urgently calling for anyone with medical skills. One was on a mobile phone calling for an ambulance. As a teacher he had basic knowledge of first aid, and offered to take a look. The group parted to let him see.

It was Jenny.

She was lying there, trying desperately to draw breath, eyes glazed, scarcely conscious, legs limp, her whole body covered in mud. Blood trickled from the corner of her mouth.

"Jenny, Jenny! It's Danny - can you hear me. I'm here, I'm here."

He knew he should not attempt to move her, but wanted to try to ease her breathing.

"Did anyone see what happened?" he asked.

"The horse rolled on to her when it slipped. She couldn't get out of the way," a woman half-sobbed.

"There's an ambulance on its way," some else said.

Danny tried to stay, calm, to hold back his tears, as he tried to make her comfortable. With his handkerchief he cleaned her ashen face, and wiped away the blood, but it still came. Her once sparkling eyes were dim and unseeing and the breaths she managed were noisy, hard-drawn and painful.

"Darling hold on, hold on. Help is coming, we'll soon have you somewhere safe."

He put his coat over her, and others offered their coats too, but they dare not risk moving her to put coats under her. They could only leave her lying on the sodden ground.

"Danny..." Jenny spoke his name with enormous effort.

"Danny...Danny!" Her voice was weak but there was a strange excitement in it as he cradled her head in the trampled mud, and gently wiped the blood that oozed from her mouth, and ran down to mingle with the wet earth, and colour it crimson. He could see only her face and her eyes – everything else going on around them was shut out.

"Jenny, don't try to talk. Just lie quietly. Help is coming. We'll get you out of here to somewhere comfortable, and someone to take a look at you. Lie quietly, my love."

But she wasn't listening, or may be it was that she wasn't hearing him.

"Danny... I can... smell the flowers... that honeysuckle... it is so strong...so...beautiful. I feel..."

Her throat choked and gurgled again, but she made a supreme effort:

"...I feel like a child again, Danny... I'm so... comfortable... so warm... I can feel that soft grass... against my face. It smells... so.. sweet... And...and..."

Her voice was weakening and fading. Danny could only stroke her pale face. He saw her only mistily through his tears.

"...and the gorse...so strong...that elixir of our youth...Do you...remember...Will it...make me...?"

Jenny's voice tailed off to an inaudible whisper. She tried vainly to turn, to reach out to touch the bright yellow of the gorse, a few feet away...

So close – yet tantalisingly out of reach from where she lay, bloodstained, crushed, her dress and her body soaked in the mud, and blood, and hate of that battleground. A beautiful woman trampled in that once beautiful place, both now mortally scarred by greed and aggression.

Her eyes closed, her breathing was scarcely discernable that day, beneath the skies of Bungay Fen, at Iris Glade, with green leaves on the silver birch and hawthorn still dancing in the windy gusts. The rain had eased at last. Not far off the cattle grazed on the Lows, unmoved by the drama. And in the sudden silence, a skylark's soaring symphony pierced the air.

Jenny opened her eyes, as if she could hear it, but unseeing. Danny took her limp hand, and felt her squeeze his, without strength. She spoke again, with a supreme effort:

"Danny…promise me this…scatter my ashes where you will…but scatter my soul in Bungay. Take me once more through its gentle streets, beneath its quaint rooftops, through St Mary's churchyard and around Holy Trinity, and every street of my wonderful town. Let me pause in each place I have loved, so that a part of each place comes with me to where I am going.

"And carry me along the Waveney at last, where the May blossom kisses the water, and where snowdrops abound in the place where George Baldry once dwelt.

"And let me see the Vineyard House once more – our house, basking in the sunshine, just across the water. Promise you will do this for me Danny…my…love…"

A long, slow, tapering sigh left Jenny's blue lips as she finished her words. Danny lifted her body and held it close to his. Tenderly he kissed her white cheek, and held his lips there.

Through the haze of his grief he heard the skylark compose another symphony.

A Requiem for Jenny.

CHAPTER FIFTEEN

GROUPS of people still remained, at a distance, most of them silent. Danny remained there too, when the ambulance had gone - stunned, shocked, unable to focus his thoughts, except on Jenny. She had been snatched from him at the very moment she seemed to have come back to him, on Outney Fen - their place, their haven, where they had nurtured their love and their plans. But it was a place which had come between them, and he hated himself for that.

But why had this tragedy happened? It had happened, he was convinced through his grief, because a group of anarchists who probably knew little about the Fen or what it stood for, decided to vent their aggression against authority. He felt certain they were not Bungay people - they had probably never been there until that morning. But they were probably also the ones he had seen an age ago outside the Fisher Theatre before one of the many meetings on the future of the Fen.

As he stood there at the spot where Jenny had died he looked up at the skies for solace, and around him to each distance part of Outney Fen. The sky was beginning to clear - there were even patches of blue sky appearing. But he shivered with the cold of his soaked body, his shock and inner pain, and loss.

His eyes took in the copse of silver birches planted to commemorate the Silver Jubilee of Queen Elizabeth II. Standing there were the bulk of the mob who he has seen charge the crowd, the mob that had caused the chaos and crush. The mob that had caused Jenny's death.

Suddenly intense anger arose in Danny's breast. He turned and strode towards them as they stood there, and as he moved his foot knocked against something in the mud. It was a police truncheon dropped during the frightening melee just a few minutes earlier. He picked it up. The group was smoking, shrugging, as the police cordoned off the area where Jenny had lain and began their investigations. They looked sheepish as he approached.

"You bastards! You murderers! You scum!"

Danny's anger came out in a half shout, half sob, as he got close to them and glared furiously at the group, still wearing their woolly hats and scarves.

"You killed my Jenny! You caused her death, you robbed me off her, and I'll see you hang for her!"

Somehow he stopped himself from lunging at the nearest of them as he stood, shaking almost uncontrollably and pointing at them.

"You know nothing about the Common, you know nothing about what this fight is about! you're anarchists - the scum of the earth..."

"Look mate, we're here because we've a right to be here, and were here to fight the capitalists who take land and other fings from people to make their millions. They're the bastards and the scum, not us. Don't you forget that."

"Don't kid yourself. You've got no idea what you're fighting or why you're fighting. You're just fired by hate of anyone that has something you haven't. You're spineless cowards and you murdered that girl and you're not even bothered about it."

"The Green Land Protection Unit regrets that there has been loss of life in this instance. It's not something we plan for and not something we like to see," said another of the group, speaking almost in a monotone.

"But this is a fight for down-trodden people of this country against people who grab all the wealth and keep it for themselves while others starve."

"So you're not protecting green land then?"

Yea, that too. Whatever."

"You've got no interest in this common - none! It's just the latest place for you to get angry about, somewhere else for you to go on your State handouts. You'll move on somewhere else tomorrow and forget about this fight. You're pathetic, you're scum and you're murderers!"

"From what we 'ear you forgot about this place too - didn't have the bo'le for the fight, did yer, did yer, did yer?"

The bedraggled speaker jabbed his finger constantly towards Danny as he screwed up his eyes and mouth into an ugly, violent scowl as he uttered the words. His finger might as well have been a knife as the words cut through Danny's conscience, and he raised his arm, scarcely realising the truncheon was still in his hand, and lunged forward in his anguish, intent in that brief moment in time on striking a fatal blow.

"You bastard! I'll show you what fight is…I'll…"

"OK Danny, it's not worth it - leave it."

Danny wheeled round as he felt a restraining arm on his shoulder. He went to strike out at whoever it was, until he realised it was Fenny.

"Come on, they're not worth it - leave it Danny," he said again gently. "Come on, I'll take you home."

Danny looked at him, stood his ground for a few moments and glared back at the mob in their anarchist uniforms - a dark, forbidding, sinister unstable group. He raised his arm again and made to move towards them…

Then he hung his head and sobbed as he allowed Fenny to shepherd him away, back towards the towered town now feeling the warm of the early morning sun as the clouds continued to melt away.

But he did not see it - his mind could only see Jenny's face as she lay in the mud and the rain and the turmoil and the hate that had taken her vibrant life.

"What have I done?" he repeated, brokenly.

Much of the rest of the day was a blur to Danny. Fenny took him to his own home, feeling that he needed to be with someone rather than on his own, and he did not have the mental strength to resist. Gwen Skipper made him a cup of coffee and offered sympathy, but there was little either of them could do except let him know that they were there, and offer the friendship, and the sort of genuine concern they were known for fondly throughout Bungay.

Danny thanked them. He sat in the conservatory which had a beautiful view of Stow Fen - the house was situated on the side of the valley out towards Flixton, and you could see over to the other side of the valley, with the Vineyard Hills in the distant back ground.

But his tormented mind could only focus in an un-co-ordinated way on the events of the day, seeing them through a haze of rain and flying hooves and angry faces and black scars in the face of the Fen. But in the centre of it all was always Jenny's face, pale and hurt, eyes dull, their liveliness gone - their life gone.

And he could only blame himself - he had deserted her, deserted Bungay, deserted the Fen, deserted the cause he had known was right and just. And who knows what might have happened had he kept behind the campaign - they might have won further delays, further time, time to make public what he had discovered about the fictional Yvonne Delgardo. The events of that morning might never had happened if he had stuck with it.

And Jenny would have been alive.

He felt ashamed, desolate, and he could not stop his tears flowing frequently. And the words of Chateaubriand about his beloved Charlotte haunted him through his grief:

"It was has if I had lost her for a second time, in the island on which I had lost her the first."

Fenny and Gwen looked in on him periodically, concerned and compassionate, to see if he wanted to talk. But they didn't press him, realising it was too early. And he couldn't eat anything.

During the afternoon he slept fitfully at last in the chair, but in his half-dreams the same images were there.

In one, he saw Jenny, seemingly miraculously alive, helped up by an old man with a beard, carrying a staff in one hand, and lead her away, with a reproachful, staring backward glance toward him as he stood there. He tried to run after them but his legs were heavy and he found himself up to his waist in water and mud, making no progress.

It was about six o'clock in the evening when Danny fully awoke, and for the first time began to focus his mind more sharply. He thought of Jenny's words as she lay in the mud and the rain, and he suddenly knew he had to get out in the air, to force himself to go back to the Fen, to walk where Jenny walked - to take her soul once more through all her favourite places. He should do that, on his own - not as part of some funeral cortege. That would be impossible anyway.

He got up, had a quick superficial wash, and went though to the living room where Fenny and Gwen were sitting watching television.

"I need to go out for some fresh air, I need to walk," he said dully.

"Don't you want anything to eat - you must eat something," said Gwen, beginning to get out of her chair.

"No, really, I'm just not hungry. But thank you - and thanks for bringing me here and looking after me so well. I don't know what I'd have done otherwise. I really am grateful."

"Think nothing of it," said Fenny. "Such an awful tragedy, awful tragedy."

"Well come back here for some supper, won't you?"

"Thank you, but I ought to get home - Megan will be in a state, and there are other things I need to do. I'll be alright. I need to be at school tomorrow."

He took his leave, and left Fenny and Gwen with concern for him in their faces. He went home and collected a relieved and excited Megan. The evening was sunny, and the warmth had a freshness about it following the heavy rain of the previous 24 hours, as Danny made his way through the town, past all the features he and Jenny had loved so well. At each he stopped and dwelt for a few moments, catching her vibrancy in his mind and offering a silent prayer for her soul - St Mary's Church, and the churchyard where each season showed its beauty in the trees, shrubs and flowers, from the blossoms of spring, through the shimmering summer to the bronzes of autumn and the snowcovered winter; and opposite the old Guildhall, which gave the street much of its atmosphere; to the Butter Cross, sitting like a plump, benign octopus as sentinel in the Market Place - Jenny's description that Danny now recalled; through to the ancient Bigod's Castle where they had strolled so often; and then into Earsham Street, lined with old buildings, its roof tops higgledy-piggledy, its colours varied, its presence relaxing.

He journeyed along Outney Road and to the Fen, via the bypass bridge, where he hesitated. Should he, could he, make that trip so soon? But his emotions were running high, he felt so close to her, almost not believing that she was dead, and the Fen meant so much to them - that land that would now be lost forever to modern development, and noise and artificial creations.

He crossed the bridge as the sun moved lower in the evening sky towards the Vineyard Hills. He could already see the spot, at the high point, where Jenny died doing her job, not even protesting outwardly. It was still cordoned off by police tape and a lone constable stood guard over it - clearly there were more investigations to be done at the site before building work could resume.

Danny approached it slowly. The constable recognised him, and out of respect said nothing - there was nothing he could say that would relieve the pain and the grief at that moment, and he withdrew some paces as Danny knelt beside the cordon. Already the sun had dried the area considerably and had turned the caked mud from black to a lighter grey in its confused pattern of ruts and tufts and lines. Horses hooves and footprints could clearly be seen at that once clamouring and noisy scene, now silent and deserted.

Apart from Jenny's soul.

"Darling Jenny…I know you're close - I can feel you, just as we always felt the presence of God when we walked here, so many times, you and I…in this beautiful sanctuary…our place of renewal. If only you could be renewed now, and we could walked hand in hand, just once more, through the gorse and the trees, beside the sweet river; if we could see the barn owls and the herons and the kingfishers together one more time…"

Danny's words were silent, through his tears, as he raised his head and looked around at the Fen scene made hazy in his grief.

"…but I will walk for you my darling - you will always be beside me here whenever I am, in my mind and in my heart…I will see your gentle face, see your soft hair move in the breeze, talk to you in the way we always talked, laugh with you…love you. And God will be with us always.

"I'm so sorry I let you down, Jenny - that I deserted you when I should have been fighting beside you. And now it's too late…too late. What have I done?"

Danny's head sunk back to his chest in his uncontrollable grief, and he was aware of nothing around him, of no sound.

Yet, suddenly, there was a sound, and Danny raised his face to the evening sky.

The soaring skylark was composing another symphony - clear, bright, vibrant. Challenging whoever heard it.

At that moment, in the quietness, It was almost as if it was a message from Jenny.

For some time Danny knelt there, seeing little, thinking much, as the sun sank towards the Vineyard Hills and the shadows of the gorse and the scrub oaks lengthened. Soon the shadows of the hills would cast a night-time shroud over the Fen, over that fatal spot.

Eventually Danny stood up, his prayers exhausted. He nodded towards the police officer, standing as still as a heron after landing, and made for the bottom of the Fen.

He went through the curtain of silver birch, into Iris Glade and down to the bridge, still on his mission to complete Jenny's final request. He stopped there for a few moments, looking down into the water, and then climbed the stile onto the Lows. The grazing marshes were still just in the sunshine as he made his way along the river bank, to the point opposite Vineyard House, snuggling into the hills, clad in its Suffolk pink under its neatly thatched roof. The house they had dreamed of owning, one day. A dream that had died with Jenny. But Danny knew it was one of those places where her soul would freely wander.

He moved on, along Waveney's bank. Glancing to the south he saw the tower of St Mary's, the lowering sun giving it an orange glow from that distance. And closer, a barn owl began his systematic sortie of the meadows. Danny passed Finches Well, Ditchingham Lodge on the opposite side of the river, and then Sandy, where they had swum and sunbathed and enjoyed the sight of green chestnut trees against the blue sky.

He lingered there too, remembering, before turning back and retracing his steps around the Lows and back to the bridge. This time he stayed there for several moments, with his thoughts in the twilit quietness. His heart was heavy, and suddenly an almost uncontrollable anger overt took his grief and he turned his head and glared towards the darkening sky.

"Pontius Pilate took your Son. I have tried to shake off his shackle from me – to do it differently, to make the strong decision. And what happens? You still take my Jenny from me. My lovely…beautiful…gentle…treasure.

What have I done? Tell me what you want me to do! TELL ME! Shall I be Judas next?"

He was shouting out loud in the twilight, hands raised, eyes looking to the sky, and the final words were drawn out in a crescendo of despair. His voice echoed slightly over the grazing meadows where a vaporous mist was beginning to form and the legs of the cattle statues disappeared into it.

Then there was just the sound of silence. There was no answer to his challenging cries. Danny's head dropped into his hands as he leant on the rails of the bridge and looked into the stagnant dyke beneath, his mind empty, his eyes unseeing.

Suddenly he opened his eyes and saw the dark water in front of him. A violent dark.

"I could have killed that man today! I really could have killed him!"

He was talking in his head.

"I had that truncheon in my hand, and I had hate and violence in my heart - I could have beaten that chap to death. I wanted to. At that moment I wanted to beat him and beat him and beat him senseless. I wanted to murder him!"

A shiver ran through his body as the word leapt to the front of his mind - a peaceful man, yet capable of murder, albeit in the extreme circumstance of high emotion brought about by the death of someone he loved deeply. He could have done it, if Fenny had not been there to stop him. The emotion of anger and revenge was there, somewhere in his soul, and had come to the forefront of his mind, released through his grief.

Yes, yes, I could have done it - would have done it but for Fenny. What an awful, awful thought."

He stayed like that for several minutes, closing his eyes over the dark water and dark thoughts. Megan, as always, sat patiently beside him, head on one side, eyes alert, waiting for movement from her master.

"Come on Meg – let's go home."

Finally her master did move, and she eagerly went on ahead of him, beside the high grass, towards the town.

As he moved through the belt of trees he was suddenly aware of a shadowy figure standing beside one of the silver birches, its white bark, even in the dark, almost reflecting an ethereal aura on to his ghostly, bearded face.

The figure seemed to take a step forward.

"Peter? Peter? No…you're not Peter, are you."

And just as suddenly the bearded figure, carrying a staff, was gone into the darkness, leaving every nerve in Danny's body tingling with fear.

It was that same man he had seen once before, and still searching for Peter, who ever he was.

Danny hurried on, an uncomfortable feeling in his spine as he felt sinister figures could be just behind him. Thank goodness Megan was with him.

A huge feeling of relief wafted over him as he finally reached the kissing gate and crossed the bypass into Broad Street.

CHAPTER SIXTEEN

DANNY made his way back to the town, not wanting to leave the sheltering dusk and the Common, unable to form in his mind any plan for the next day - unable to look to a future without Jenny.

Through Broad Street, past the Fisher Theatre, and on through the Market Place and into Trinity Street he made his way, heavy-legged and slowly.

He passed the gates of Holy Trinity Church, and then on an impulse stopped. No - the church would be closed now, the doors were always locked at 8pm and it was now nearly 8.45pm. Yet he felt impelled to check.

It was still open. There was a knack to lifting the latch on the heavy oak door, reinforced with iron studwork, but he was familiar with it, and was quickly in the cool of the church, beside the stone font. He had not noticed it through the window, but there was a light still on at the east end, over the chancel, giving the nave an eerie yet welcoming spiritual glow, and highlighting the brass cross on its central position on the altar.

Danny fixed his gaze on it as he moved slowly down the aisle, and knelt in front of it at the altar rails. There was a heavy aura of sanctity in that sacred place, a perfect peace enfolding him, and he was alone in the presence of God.

He prayed for Jenny's soul, thanked God for taking her into his kingdom, prayed for those grieving for her, asked for forgiveness for letting her down, for help and guidance in coping with his grief, for the strength of mind to go on, for courage in the actions he had to take over the coming weeks and months.

He fixed his eyes on the cross again, and then to the east window. The butterfly was there again - it seemed to be there at every service, fluttering back and forth in its constant search for freedom, never giving up the fight.

He still knelt, holding on to the altar rail, suddenly feeling exhausted. He eyes wandered to the small window on the north side of the aisle, with its stained glass figures of young people in otherwise clear diamond panes. One was the young David, with a lamb at his side. The other was a kneeling child, the young Jesus, looking upwards, with the words above his head - Learn of Me. And beneath him another scroll: A Thank Offering from the Infant Sunday School.

Week in, week out, the children had given their pennies, back in the early 1950s. It seemed an impossible task in those days to raise the £100 it then cost, but their infant faith was unwavering, encouraged by their teachers, and the unveiling of the window brought new light to the choir stalls and joy to the church congregation of all ages.

Danny looked at the faces in the window, depicted surrounded by an aura of light. The face of the younger one was raised heavenward, and the expression in his eyes was one of absolute faith, unquestioning, unwavering, loving, devout.

As he studied it, the butterfly fluttered across the window, and landed momentarily on the stained glass. With the last vestiges of the sunset coming through the colours and the soft light inside the nave, the aura of God's presence in that intimate church was heightened still further. As he had often felt on the Fen, Danny sensed he was so close to Him in that moment.

He turned his face to the altar cross again, and offered a prayer of thanks, before standing up. On his way out of the church, he paused at the open Bible on the lectern - a large, illustrated and illuminated copy used at every service for the reading of the lessons and psalms.

It was open at St Matthew's Gospel, chapter 16, and as he scanned it, one verse caught his eye:

"And I say unto thee, that thou art Peter, and upon this rock I will build My church. And the gates of hell shall not prevail against it."

It was that name again.

Back at home, Jenny's face smiled at Danny from the photo frame on the chest of drawers as he prepared for bed and she was foremost in his mind as he lay in the dark. He went through in his mind the good times they had enjoyed, the work they had done together, the help and encouragement they had given each other in their respective jobs, and the love they had shared at last.

The grief was raw - but through it he was able to begin to form plans for the days ahead.

The morning papers were full of the story of what had happened at Outney Fen, with graphic pictures of the scenes preceding Jenny's death. The Gazette had a picture of her which filled most of the front page, under a headline: Jenny of the Gazette - Killed doing the Job She Loved.

Radio and television bulletins also covered the tragedy in depth and Danny could not prevent the tears flowing again as he heard and read the glowing tributes from editors and civic leaders to her work and integrity and objective reporting, to her love of Bungay, and of the common where she died.

As he read the press reports he forced down a cup of coffee, barely tasting it. Pilgrim's boss George Bell was quoted in the Gazette.

"No words from me can ease the grief her family and colleagues will be feeling at this tragic accident. All I can say is that the heartfelt sympathy of myself personally and everyone at Pilgrim's goes out to them. This is a tragedy that was not meant to happen, which should not have happened, and one which I believe was brought about directly or indirectly by the actions of a few lawless hooligans.

"Because of the police investigations work on the Iris Glade project will be held up for a day or two, but as a mark of respect I have decided that it will be suspended for three weeks, until after Miss Roger's funeral has taken place and to give a due time for her loved ones to revisit the place once it is free of restrictions.

"From the interviews I had with Miss Rogers I found her polite, considerate, forceful but fair - a credit to her profession and to her newspaper. Should there be any plans in Bungay for a memorial to her, my company will be prepared to contribute generously to the cost.

"This is a sad day for Bungay, for us as a company at an event which should have been a celebration of a project to which we are still fully committed, but most of all of course for Miss Roger's family and close friends."

It was the sort of statement Danny would have expected from him - a public relations statement from a man experienced at saying the right thing for the public to hear. And he was right about what brought about Jenny's death.

But he was pleased with the three-week moratorium on the work - that time would be a valuable breathing space in which to speak to people.

The telephone rang. It was Bill Burdock, the editor of the Gazette, who apologised for the early call.

"I didn't want to call yesterday Danny, and I hope you don't mind me calling today. Do tell me immediately if you are not ready to talk about this awful tragedy - I will understand completely and will leave it alone. But I know how close you and Jenny were, and she had no close family. I wanted to give you an opportunity to tell us your feelings if you felt up to it."

"No that's OK Bill, I know you have a job to do. I'm still numb obviously, but there are things I want to say, things I plan to do that I want people to know about."

He paused, and Bill said: "Do you want to tell me now, or shall I come and see you - I can easily do that?"

Danny took a deep breath:

"Jenny was a fighter, Bill - she had a quiet but steely determination that belied her gentleness. I know the Gazette will miss her terribly - I will miss her terribly, and Bungay will miss her terribly, she did so much for the town, through her work and in many other ways.

"The fact is…" Danny was fighting to stay in control of his emotions. "…the fact is, she would still be alive if I had had the same belief and unshakable conviction that she had over this Fen thing. I blame myself for what happened…no,.no, its true Bill - " as the editor tried to contradict him - "no, I'm not going to gloss over it. If I'd stayed with it, continued to fight, that event on the Fen yesterday morning - God, was it really only yesterday? - it would never have happened. I let Jenny down, I let everyone down, for what I now know were misguided reasons."

"Danny, you don't know that - and what happened yesterday might well have happened at a later date if not then…"

"Yes, but we don't know that either. Anyway, what you can say is that I am taking up the fight again, on Jenny's behalf. We can't let her death count for nothing - I don't intend to do that. This is by no means finished yet Bill, by no means. And I'll start by giving you some information I gave Jenny a few minutes before she died - that woman who spoke so convincingly at the inquiry wasn't Yvonne Delgardo at all. There is no such person. She was a professional actress - Gabriella Collingwood."

Bill Burdock drew an audible breath.

"My God, are you sure? If you're saying the developers deliberately misled the inquiry that is quite an accusation."

"That is what I'm saying Bill - I saw her in London, in a show. She has never lived in Beccles or anywhere near here, and she doesn't have a family. What she is, so I'm told, is one if this country's most promising actresses, and she certainly showed that at the inquiry. There must be a story for you there."

"Hmmm, could be, but we'd have to do some research and make some inquiries to be sure of our ground. Are you prepared to be quoted on this if necessary?"

"Certainly am. I owe it to Jenny to take up the campaign again and this is a good start - it could lead to the inquiry decision being overturned, couldn't it?"

"Possibly - I'm not clear on the legal implications of lying to an inquiry, and procuring some one to lie to it, which is what Pilgrim's have done if what you say is true. But at the very least it would surely be looked at as a serious matter by the planning inspectorate, I'm sure."

"That woman deceived me to the extent that I dropped my opposition to something I knew in my heart of hearts was wrong, and I've paid for it with Jenny's life, Bill…her life. How can I rest without doing something to try to atone for that?"

"OK, I know Danny, but don't blame yourself too much on that - she clearly deceived most of the people at the inquiry that day, including the inspector, though I doubt that what she had to say had that much sway on his decision. There were many other things to be taken into account on a much more practical front. But if I run a story we'll have to keep it balanced and in perspective, and Pilgrim's will bring their lawyers down heavily on us at the least excuse."

"I'll stand by everything I say about it. There is no doubt that Yvonne Delgardo was not Yvonne Delgardo."

"OK, leave it with me. As far as the campaign is concerned, if it is to continue, keep me informed Danny, and the Gazette will continue to give it coverage."

"Well, there are others running the campaign now as you know - I'll let them know I'm back on board and talk to them about a few ideas I have to take it forward to keep it in the spotlight, but I guess they will continue to lead it for the time being."

Bill nodded, and added: "Personally, if there is anything I can do to help you at a time like this, do let me know. I know at the moment anything I can say won't help much, but you do have my great sympathy, and that goes for everyone at this office."

"I know Bill - I do appreciate that. One thing you can help me with - do you know who will be organising Jenny's funeral? Close as I was too her, she never spoke much about her relatives, and as you know she lost both parents when she was still in her teens."

"That I can help with - she had an uncle who was her closest relative and he's taking over the arrangements. Just a tick, I've got his number here somewhere."

After speaking to Bill Burdock, Danny spent the next hour or so making a number of phone calls and writing a number of letters to a variety of people in Bungay and around the area, nationally, and even abroad, as he followed up new ideas which had formed in his mind to take forward the Save Our Fen campaign.

He was by no means sure what effect they would have and indeed how practical they were - they would depend on a number of outside influences, including nature. But he was encouraged by the calls he made that they would be worth trying, even in challenging someone as seemingly intransigent as George Bell and his corporation.

Focussing on practical matters and talking to people made Danny feel better in mind and spirit, and gave him a renewed resolve. At lunch-time he ate something for the first time since Jenny had died.

And he had to return to school - it was almost the end of the summer term, with school events reaching a climax. He had taken a couple of days off, but Danny owed it to the rest of the staff and the children to return, and he had to get back to some semblance of normality.

His colleagues on the staff knew how close he had been to Jenny, and they offered their sympathy when he went into the staff room of the Victorian, ivyclad school. The atmosphere was subdued, but businesslike, and they updated him on end of term matters.

He was glad to get into the classroom again, to the excited chatter of seven-year-olds hyped by the knowledge that the summer holidays were not far way. They would barely be aware of what had happened on the Fen, and it was just as well, Danny thought - better that they remembered it as the place where he had taken them on nature walks, for projects on birds, or to see how many different flowers and grasses they could identify.

When the break time bell went he dismissed them and there was a hubbub of chatter as they made for the door to get out into the sunshine and expend their pent-up energy in their playground games.

As Danny sat and watched them go as he tidied books, one child lingered, as if she wanted to say something but was too shy to do so. It was Chloe.

"Do you want to tell me something, Chloe?" Danny inquired gently.

The little girl in her sky blue summer uniform dress, covered by a long dark ponytail down her back, blushed:

"Mummy said…she said she's sorry about your girlfriend." She blurted out the last few words in a hurry.

Danny was taken aback, but he smiled and said: "Thank you Chloe."

"Mummy said she's gone to heaven."

"Mummy's quite right Chloe - she has. And no harm can come to her ever again."

"Mr Tegerdine…Mr Tegerdine, what is heaven like? My Mummy says it is like a big garden."

"Well, I suppose it is a bit like that. I believe it is a beautiful place, very peaceful, with lots of flowers and trees. A bit like the Fen maybe."

"Will your girlfriend stay on the Fen now she's dead," Chloe said, more boldly now.

Danny winced inwardly, and thought for a moment before he said:

"Chloe, my Jenny was a good person and she loved the Fen, and when I think of her I will imagine her there. I think the Fen was her heaven."

"Yes. Mr Tegerdine. But...but, Mummy says they are going to dig the Fen up, so she won't be able to be there, will she?"

A lump was forming in Danny's throat as he replied: "Well Chloe, we'll have to try to make sure they don't dig it up, so everyone can still go there."

"I love the Fen, Mr Tegerdine. I don't want them to dig it up. Can you stop them, can you? Please, please stop them Mr Tegerdine. Please."

There was a long pause before Danny managed to say:

"I will do my very, very best, Chloe. I love it too."

"Thank you, Mr Tegerdine."

And for the first time, a huge smile broke out on the child's previously serious face as her childlike trust manifested itself. She hesitated, before running off after her friends.

There was a mistiness in Danny's eyes as he watched her go. He had not noticed it before, but suddenly he realised that Chloe, with her wide brown eyes and sudden smile, bore a striking resemblance to Jenny.

CHAPTER SEVENTEEN

THE heavy summer rain returned a week later, saturating the Fen, leaving huge puddles along Bungay's main street and that delicate, energising freshness that comes when rain drops fall on arid paving slabs.

And it fell on the funeral cortege carrying the coffin of Jenny Rogers to Holy Trinity Church, and on the many mourners who made their way there to pay their last tributes to her on that July day. The rain on the windows of the hearse seemed to become symbolic teardrops in memory of a woman who had brightened many lives.

Holy Trinity was full for the service, with extra chairs put out in the Lady Chapel. Even so, some were left standing at the back, around the font, and even in the porch. The town Reeve of Bungay, and the Mayor were there - and Danny spotted George Bell and his company secretary towards the back of the main aisle.

As the coffin was carried in the strains of Moon River, one of Jenny's favourite songs, accompanied it. Danny could not help thinking how poignant for the occasion were the words from it: "...dream maker, you heart breaker, wherever you're going, I'm going your way..."

Her journey though life had been cut off so prematurely.

Jenny's uncle, Charles Rogers, had asked Danny to pay the tribute address at the service, and he had readily accepted. He knew what he had to say and what he had to do.

At the appointed time in the service he stood before the lectern, his heart thumping with nervousness. He spoke of Jenny's childhood, growing up in the Stour valley in the south of Suffolk, of her love of the rural surroundings, of her gift of writing which she had nurtured almost from the time she could spell, of her outgoing nature, her kindness, compassion, her Christian faith - and her determination to stand up and battle for what she thought was right.

"Those of you who did not know Jenny directly as a person will have known her through her writing for the Gazette. The family have asked me, on their behalf, to thank all of you for your messages and letters of sympathy. All of us here so wish we did not have to be here in these circumstances, we so wish that such a tragedy had not struck her down in the way it did. But Jenny would have said, in the way she did, that that was God's will, or her destiny.

"As you know, Jenny loved Bungay Fen, and she loved her work - and she died doing the job she loved, in the place she loved, and we must all try to feel that that is some consolation as we grieve for her."

Danny paused, and took a deep breath before addressing the hushed congregation again:

"I have mentioned her determination. One thing she was determined about, and worked hard, and fairly, for through her work, was that the Fen should remain untouched, as a recreation, golfing and grazing area. She was unable to say that openly as a personal view because of her work, but now I can say it for her, and I owe it to her to say it. She would have wanted me to say it, here, in this place at this service: Bungay Fen, and Iris Glade, must remain as they are."

He paused again, and looked directly at George Bell: "Those of us here who loved Jenny and love the Fen must work to see that this is Jenny's legacy, that her death there is not wasted. I hope somehow, Jenny can know that I am saying that and, Mr Bell, we all plead with you once more, even at this late stage in the process."

He raised his voice, now slightly shaky with emotion, and it rang loud and clear through the pillars and the pews and aisles of the old Saxon church:

"Please, for her sake if no one else's, drop this housing scheme. Please listen to the voices of Bungay, please. You Mr Bell, have cheated us once already by providing false evidence at the inquiry...yes, Mr Bell," as he saw the big man start to rise angrily from his seat, "yes you did, through Yvonne Delgardo, who does not exist as that person, does she? You got an actress to do your dirty work for you, and she was so good at it that she convinced the inspector, and me and many other people! You cheated us all to help get your scheme through. She did a fine job for you - I hope you paid her well!"

George Bell was now fully on his feet and the stunned and startled congregation, after a few moments to take in what they heard, broke into a hubbub of loudly whispered chatter and movement, and turned their eyes to fix them on the stout corporate and corpulent chairman.

Furiously red in the face, he snarled down the aisle at Danny, still standing firmly at the lectern: "That is a serious accusation and one you will pay very dearly for, Mr Tegerdine. You will be hearing from my solicitor very shortly."

As he and his company secretary stormed towards the church door, they stopped and turned momentarily, and there was silence again as Danny said, steadfastly:

"Mr Bell, the plea goes with you. It is Jenny's plea. I knows the words you have heard today will remain in your mind and find their way to your heart."

Mr Bell said nothing, and left. A subdued hubbub returned, until Danny said: "I apologise to those of you who may feel this has been the wrong place to say these things, but I don't apologise for saying them. We are here to pay tribute to Jenny, to remember her and what she stood for. I know she will be happy with what has been said.

"Personally I feel I have let her down once. I don't intend to let her down again. That is my pledge to someone I loved and admired, and I know many of you did too."

Danny bowed his head slightly, stood a moment longer at the lectern, and made his way back to his seat.

As he did so, someone started to clap, others tentatively took it up.

By the time he had reached his seat, the old church resounded to sustained applause. As he sat down, out of the corner of his eye he noticed the butterfly still fluttering determinedly against the east window.

Next day the Gazette and other papers carried prominent stories on the funeral service and its dramatic happenings. Bill Burdock had been there, with a senior reporter, who had spoken to Danny afterwards, and quoted him as saying he would stand by his accusations and provide evidence if necessary. The details of his encounter with actress Gabriella Collingwood, and her background, were also incorporated into the story. Ominously to Danny, the Gazette had contacted her agent and he had said his client did not wish to comment on the accusation.

George Bell was also quoted, repeating his response in church that it was a disgraceful accusation which demeaned the occasion, and that Mr Tegerdine would be hearing shortly from his solicitor.

That letter was delivered by hand to Danny's house later that day. It read:

Dear Mr Tegerdine,

I refer to comments made by you at Holy Trinity Church, Bungay, on July 18th, 2007, during the funeral service for Miss Jenny Rogers.

My client Mr George Bell, of Pilgrims Plc, has asked me to write to you urgently calling on you to immediately and publicly withdraw the accusations you made again him - namely, that comments made by Yvonne Delgardo were not made by her, but by an actress employed to portray her in her role as a single mother.

I have advised my client that should such an apology not appear in the Waveney Gazette within the next seven days that, on his behalf, I will issue a writ for damages against you on the grounds of defamation of character. My client completely and without reservation denies the unsubstantiated allegations you made against him on the date and place named above.

Furthermore, he is concerned that the allegations were made in the way they were at such an event, and that the memory of Miss Jenny Rogers was greatly demeaned by them.

I await your urgent reply.

Yours sincerely,

J R Harper,

Spraggs, Knight and Simpson

Danny read the Gazette and the solicitor's letter with some anxiety, and a little anger. If Gabriella Collingwood and her agent were not prepared to admit anything, and George Bell continued to claim his allegations were unsubstantiated, there seemed to be little he could do to pursue what he had been told and claim the inquiry decision should be overturned.

That evening he sat in his garden in the evening sunshine, looking through the beauty of the silver birch nearby to the evening sky as its azure blue dimmed and gradually took on its ephemeral pink and orange and purple evening hue. He and Jenny had often sat together and enjoyed one of nature's remarkable transformations, but he could not concentrate on it as he tried to sort out in is mind what he could do.

Perhaps he should write a letter of apology to George Bell's solicitors, and one to Bill Burdock for use in the letters columns of the Gazette, to close the matter, if he was going to be unable to substantiate what he had been told in London. He had been over emotional when he had made his statement at the funeral, and perhaps he had been unfair, even to someone like George Bell, to put him on the spot like that, when everyone should have been concentrating on the memory of Jenny. He needed to get the issue behind him quickly, so he could pursue other ways of fighting the Iris Glade scheme, even at this late stage.

But the solicitor's letter has also angered him - for George Bell, of all people, to claim that what he, Danny, had said had demeaned the memory of Jenny. What on earth right had he to say something like that? What did he know about Jenny and what she stood for, and what she meant to people? It was almost an unsubstantiated allegations against him?

Danny stood up and strode to the end of the garden and back as his anger grew. Why should he think of apologising to a man like that?

Next morning, however, came another set back, to a move he had set considerable hope by. It was a letter form the Government's Planning Inspectorate, based in Bristol:

Dear Mr Tegerdine:

Thank you for your letter of July 14th. The accusation you make against Pilgrim Plc, which has put forward the plan for Bungay common which was the subject of a planning inquiry in Bungay last year, is a most serious one.

However you included nothing, other than your statement of what you were told by the agents of Miss Gabriella Collingwood, to substantiate your claim, and it is not the role of the Planning Inspectorate to carry out investigations into such matters without very good reason for doing so.

I have to tell you that, in any event, it is unlikely that even if the claims were substantiated, it would not serve to alter the decision of the Secretary of State for the Environment, Food and Rural Affairs, at this late stage.

In such circumstances there may be a case for criminal action against Mr George Bell, as chairman of Pilgrim Plc, but that would be an entirely separate issue and would be a matter for the police.

In view of this there is no action that I propose to take on behalf of the Planning Inspectorate on this issue. The permission for the Iris Glade scheme remains unaltered. In any event, the evidence of Miss Yvonne Delgardo was only one aspect of the wide-ranging evidence the inspector took into account at the inquiry in coming to his recommendation.

I am sending a copy of this letter to the applicants for their information.

Yours sincerely,
David Shanahan,
Senior Solicitor, HM Planning Inspectorate

Danny frowned as he put the letter in his desk. So there was to be no help from the Government department that Pilgrims had conned by false evidence, and none from Gabriella Collingwood, who had been instrumental in perpetrating the deceit - all of which meant he was left in a difficult situation as far as apologising or not, to George Bell, was concerned.

"These people just don't want to know, do they Meg," he said as he sat down at the table and opened the morning paper. "They are in far away places and are just not interested in what goes on here. No doubt Gabriella got well paid for her performance - I'm not surprised she wants to lie low and not say anything. And we who have done nothing wrong, said nothing that is not accurate, are the one's having to defend ourselves and write a letter of apology to someone about to tear the heart out of a community and destroy a facility that has been part of it since Neolithic man was here. How can that be right?"

He stood up again and returned to the desk.

"There's no point in putting it off - I might as well write the letter now and get it over with. Then we'll go on the Fen, Megan - we might as well make the most of it while we've got the chance. It's not going to be there much longer."

He took out his writing pad and sat down again and wrote the letter. There was a feeling deep inside him that he should resist, but the consequences of that at the moment were dire. He just had to hope that some of his other plans would be more effective.

He took some time over the letter, and when he had finished it copied it into the computer so he could forward it to the Gazette. As he sealed the envelope and addressed it, he turned the page of the Daily Mail, on the table in front of him, and there was the face go George Bell staring at him from the business supplement.

Danny looked at it more closely. It was a profile on the man who had been born in the poorest part of London 55 years ago, with nothing, but had pulled himself up with his shoestrings through sheer hard work, got a job with a small building concern, became manager of it, through wheeler-dealing had managed to acquire a piece of building land, developed it, bought out the company he had worked for - and progressed rapidly from there. He had formed Pilgrim's 10 years previously and made it one of the most successful development companies in the UK, with sites in many parts of the country and, according to the article, provided thousands of people with the chance of owning their own home that they would otherwise not have had.

He had never forgotten his roots and the struggles of his own family to afford rent for a nondescript home. They could not even have dreamed of owning their own home, and that is what had been the driving force behind his ambitions to see that others in their position could be given the chance.

He came across in the article as a doting father, and loving grandfather - already he had six grand-daughters, and said: "I spoil them, I admit it. I just can't resist their smiles and the way they ask for things, and thank goodness I'm able to give them to them. Not everyone is in that position."

And he said: "They are my life. I've kept back one house on each of the developments I've built for one of my grandchildren, so they never have to worry about having somewhere to live."

Danny closed the paper and put it away. "That is an article that lacks any semblance of sincerity," he thought to himself.

He alerted Megan, and went up the town to post the letter. There was a postbox in St Mary's Street, outside the chemist's. He was about to put the letter through the slot when a little voice said:

"Hello Mr Tegerdine!"

He turned round in the busy street.

"Oh, hello Chloe, I didn't see you. What are you doing today?"

"Mummy's taking us for a picnic on the Fen, by the river, and we're...and we're going to paddle!"

She hesitated, and built up the courage to add, with her wonderfully trusting smile: "I told Mummy you said you wouldn't let them dig up the Fen."

And she skipped off with her family.

Danny's hand held on to the envelope in the mouth of the postbox for many seconds, his mind mixed up again.

Then he let it drop into the sack inside.

The letter of apology appeared in the letters column of The Gazette two days later. Danny had written it with a heavy heart, with Jenny very much in the forefront of his mind as he did so. He knew she would have frowned on him doing so, but he felt he had little option - and this time it did not mean he was giving up the fight. It was simply one avenue of challenge that seemed to have closed, for the moment at least, and there were still others.

Besides, he thought to himself as he re-read the letter in the paper, it was not just an apology. He also used it to highlight again the overwhelming sadness and anger there still was in Bungay about the plan - and he recounted in it his heart-tugging encounter in the classroom with Chloe, the youngest generation which would miss the wide open acres and the recreation they offered in a town which was not well provided with playground facilities.

The same edition of the newspaper carried the announcement that Pilgrim's would commence work on the development on September 1st, and this time there would be no ceremony. It outlined the tight security the company planned for the day to prevent any repetition of the tragedy which had occurred during the previous attempt to start work.

The news heartened Danny. It meant a full month of opportunity to try challenge the plan in whatever way possible, determined, controlled, but without aggression.

Two weeks later, with the school holidays in full swing, came an event which he hoped would have a moving effect even on someone as commercially orientated as George Bell. It depended much on nature and the weather being absolutely right and to Danny's huge joy, it was.

CHAPTER EIGHTEEN

"WELL, Mr Tegerdine, we're here and it may be high summer but at this time in the morning it's still damn cold, with this mist still hanging around. What exactly was it you wanted us to see?"

"In Bungay we always have a ceremony on the common to celebrate high summer - to welcome it at dawn or around dawn. That is why we have the wooden cross erected here, at the highest point, and hold a service. I wanted you to see what a special occasion it is, how important it is. It is our last chance to hold it here - your first chance to witness it."

"But there are very few people here except us - you can't have a service without people surely?"

Danny had Chloe clutching his hand as he answered;

"It's not quite time, yet – give it a couple more minutes. We're just waiting for someone, some thing. It may be cold but when it is like this at this time in the morning, around 6am, it means it is going to be a beautiful day, one of those summer days when the Fen is at its best. It's good of you to be here. How much time have you actually spent on this Fen, Mr Bell? Have you seen it in all its seasons?"

Mr Bell sighed agitatedly.

"I have not been here very often, Mr Tegerdine, but I know a lot about it –we heard it interminably at the public meeting and the planning meeting, and at the appeal inquiry. I know all the…what the devil is that?"

The works hooter from the factory on the other side of the bypass sounded out its blaring tone, summoning staff to the 6am shift, and echoing loud and clear across the Fen too – a less pleasant sound than the bells of St Mary's, but effective.

Suddenly, almost as the last echoes of the hooter died away on the still air, they gave way to another sound, barely audible at first even in the still morning air, gentle, but gradually rising. The group standing there in the middle of the common, with the morning mist at waist height, still not burned off by the early sun, around them, were startled at first, then perplexed as they looked first one way and then another, hearing the sound around them, but unable to see where it was coming from.

Even for Danny, well prepared for it, the effect was uncanny, and sent shivers down his spine as he listened to the gentle singing, unaccompanied, but gradually growing in volume, the words becoming discernable. The words of that beautiful hymn: "Lord, the light of your love is shining,

In the midst of the darkness shining...."

And as the singing increased, the mesmerised group suddenly perceived white figures rising eerily, ethereally, slowly, above the level of the morning mist, first in front of them, from the area of the plague pit 100 yards or so away, then behind them from the area of The Lows, and then on either side – more and more figures, more and more white-clad voices. And as they stood up to full height they reached the crescendo of the chorus:

"Shine, Jesus Shine fill this land with the Father's glory,

"Blaze Spirit, blaze, set our hearts on fire!

"Flow, river flow, flood the nations with grace and mercy,

"Send forth your Word, Lord and let there be light."

Now the words echoed in full volume to every corner of the common, embracing every tree, every thorn bush, every flower, every dyke and every hollow, and the river around it, calling the message in 1000 voices – the message of the land of the Father's glory, green, pleasant and peaceful.

At this moment and in this special, untouched place, that land was the Fen.

It was a ghostly, thrilling, awesome sound and sight, and Danny could almost see the hair of those in the group standing on end as they stood transfixed, watching and listening, unable to move, not knowing what to do or how to respond to such a sight on that early, shimmering morning in July – surreal, but actually happening.

The singing, remarkably in harmony, seemed to echo and rebound from the Vineyard Hills, around the petals of the water lilies beginning to open for the day on the surface of the river, through the barn owls wooded nests, touching every gorse bush, telling the message of the glory and peace of the Common, God's creation, and the constancy it stood for.

As the singing continued, the figures began to move slowly forward, on all sides, towards the group, with the mist still swirling around their feet, a deliberate movement, compelled by the strength of peace, not aggression. On they came determinedly, rhythmically, some climbing the style from the Lows, others climbing the escarpment from the west, the words still growing in volume, their steps seemingly in unison. And as they closed closely around the group the final note was held, and the warm sun burned away the final strands of mist…

"….Liiiiiiiiight!"

The massed choir fell silent, their white robes shimmering in the sunlight, their eyes fixed on the group. But because those men and women could not understand what was happening, they could not hold their gaze with their own. Instead, intimidated, they only looked guiltily at each other, or above the heads, or at the ground, and shifted their feet nervously.

The whole common was silent – except for the soaring skylark, composing another symphony, high above that scene. From her lofty view, she saw this circle of 1000 people in miniature, with the group within it a tiny central dot, a white circle in the very centre of the Fen green, stretching away around it to the river, the

Vineyard Hills to the north, the cattle statues on the Lows. A scene of perfect peace.

Danny broke the silence.

"I wanted you to hear from many voices how we feel about this place in a way that will convince you of the peace of our message and the strength of our message. I wanted you to hear how this place moves us, and what it would mean to Bungay and many other people to lose it. There are 1000 singers here but that is still just a fraction of those who plead with you to leave the Fen as it is. Let there be no more deaths here. Will you withdraw this plan?"

"Mr Tegerdine, is this all you brought us here for at this time in the morning? What a complete waste of our valuable time!"

Danny fixed his eyes unwaveringly on those of his adversary. He said quietly:

"Mr Bell, what you have seen and heard here this morning will remain in your mind, whatever you say, and I believe in time its effect will find its way to your heart. Thank you for coming. Will you listen to the choirs once more before you go?"

There was no time for the big man to reply before the voices of the white-clad choristers of all ages began singing another moving anthem beneath the early morning summer sun:

Be still for the power of the Lord is moving in this place,
He comes to cleanse and heal, to minister with grace,
No work too hard for Him, in faith receive from Him;
Be still for the power for the Lord, is moving in this place."

Again the words echoed musically around the whole Common; again there was an awed silence, full of wonder and hope, before Danny said:

"Can you say you are not moved just a little by what you see and hear around you this morning, Mr Bell - can you understand the peaceful but powerful message we are bringing: that this place is worth so much more than the multi-millions it will bring to your company; that it is a rare and precious place, a rare and precious amenity as it is?"

Again there was silence as the corporate chairman glared back at Danny, and shook his head impatiently and mockingly.

He seemed to be turning to go, when the little voice of Chloe, summoning up all her childlike courage, piped up in the still air:

"Mister…mister…well…hmm…" she put her hands nervously on her hips and looked up at the big man in front of her, and finally her pleading message came gabbling out in a hurry "...please don't take our Fen away from us. We love it. Please let us keep it, please!"

Mr Bell, looked startled. For the first time, something close to a smile passed his lips, and for the first time Danny noticed a hint of gentleness in his eyes. It was almost the look of a doting grandfather.

He squatted down on his haunches to bring him down to Chloe's level, put his hand on her tiny arm, and gently rubbed it in a re-assuring way. For a moment, it seemed he was about to say something to this earnest little girl in front of him as he looked into her eyes.

He opened his mouth, and swallowed hard.

"What's your name?" he asked.

"My name is Chloe," she said more confidently.

"Chloe? I've got a beautiful grand-daughter called Chloe," the big man said, fondly.

He remained on his haunches for a few moments more. Then he stood up, and looked at her, then at Danny, and then at the scene around him, before turning to go.

And the bird of the heavens saw the white circle open on one side, and the irregular black dot remain still for a few moments, before moving away through the gap, and off towards the town.

The singers, now warm as the sun lifted further on another shimmering July day, gathered around the wooden cross for the soltice service of hymns, prayers, readings and an address by the Rev Byron Wills, which had as its theme the beauty of God's world and the constancy of the message in Christ's teaching, and its relevance in the modern world.

Prayers were said for the Fen and its future and called for guidance for all those involved with the campaign to protect it and those planning to develop it for homes and amenities. And Jenny was remembered in those messages.

CHAPTER NINETEEN

DANNY pondered over the next few days on how effective the choral plea had been. The turn-out of singers had been impressive, particularly in view of the cold they had had to endure, in choir gowns which offered little protection, beneath the level of the mist for a good half hour before the appointed time before they could begin to sing and move. But the effect of the staged appeal had been awe-inspiring, and would have moved most people who witnessed it. But was it enough to move George Bell and his team to the extent that it would deter them from pressing ahead with the plan which had had such a tragic start?

"Realistically, no," said Danny out loud to himself, as he walked in the lea of the Vineyard Hills on his daily walk with Megan, and admired again the beauty of Vineyard House - the house he and Jenny had day-dreamed about owning one day.

"No, the stakes are too high to deter them, however emotive the event. Their mindset was wrong from the start, the timing was probably wrong. But - it was worth a try. So what's next Megan - we've got less than a month left to honour the memory of our Jenny in the way she would most want it. All this talk of a monument to her in the new development is all very well, but it will be meaningless if the plan goes ahead."

It was nearly a month since her death, but far too early to begin to come to terms with it in any meaningful way. But Danny's walks on the Fen had taken on new meaning themselves - just as he always felt close to God on the Fen, he now felt close to Jenny too, especially in Iris Glade, and he lingered there even longer than he used to, standing on the bridge, remembering their times together.

And the words of a poem he had read came into his mind, and seemed so evocative of the situation:

"And now you're there, mid silent silhouettes of scattered oaks,
Knee-deep amid the softness of the grass,
Your smile, as always, gentle on your face;
And in this time and in this pleasant place
I wish this moment now should never pass.

But Danny knew he had to move on. The only way he could do that was to find a way of preserving the Fen as it was, to stave off for ever the development plan. And he was no nearer achieving that, despite the efforts so far. George Bell seemed intransigent - or was it just the hard commercial world he was in that was intransigent, the market forces which always had a cogent and compelling reason for pushing forward financially lucrative plans?

It was too late to change the minds of the Fen Wardens - he had written individual letters to all of them, and those that had replied had made it clear the deal was done - signed and sealed. The Fen had already been sold and was now owned by Pilgrim Plc. The planning permission was still unaltered despite Danny's revelation that Yvonne Delgardo's evidence was completely false, and work was set to start, without ceremony, on September 1.

The Save Our Fen Action Group was still doing all it could - the SOF posters that had been produced more than a year ago were still up in the windows, or on posts in the gardens, of virtually every home in the town, and in a few shops, though many shops were tacitly supporting the plan as they saw it as the saviour of their struggling businesses. A regular vigil in the town centre, with placards and speeches, was still held weekly on a Saturday, but numbers at it were gradually dwindling and the police were anxious to see it end because of the regular traffic disruption in the town centre at a busy time.

It seemed there were only two possibilities left, Danny said to himself. One was to change the mind of George Bell and Pilgrim, which seemed a forlorn hope - despite his softened re-action to Chloe's plea.

The other was a long shot - intervention by the Societe Internationale au Memoir de Compte Francois de Chateaubriand.

The society, based in France, in the village in Normandy which took the Compte's name, was one of those Danny had written to as he sought every avenue of support. He and Jenny had often talked of Chateaubriand's love affair with Charlotte Ives as they had walked on the Fen, and it gave them something of a feeling of the Fen's history knowing that they were walking in the footsteps of those two who had shared the same intimate conversations in that same, beautiful place more than 200 years beforehand.

He had not been aware of the society and its aims and objects until he came upon it by chance while searching the internet on his computer. He discovered that it was more than 100 years old, and had been founded to promote the memory of the great French statesman and writer, to appreciate his writing, organise visits to his home town and others in France and throughout Europe where he had lived, such as the French Embassy in London. It was clearly an organisation of some influence, Danny judged, and a look at the names of some of its leading members showed that many were of considerable wealth.

Clearly they must know of Chateaubriand's association with Bungay and his convalescence there, he had thought. It was unlikely that they had heard of the threat to the Fen, and in any event would not be aware of Chateaubriand's time spend on it. But if they were made aware of it could they, would they, be prepared to bring their influence to bear on its future use, even at this late stage?

A reply from the society's secretary, Antoinette Clemency, gave Danny some hope. Her letter said that many year's ago, in the 1930s, a visit to Bungay by its members had taken place. They had visited the Ives former home in Bridge Street, the churches, including those in the surrounding Saints villages where the Rev John Ives had been parson, and other places in Bungay, Beccles and Great Yarmouth with which Chateaubriand had been associated after fleeing England to escape the French Revolution.

But Mme Clemency said they were not aware of his particular association with the Fen, and were interested to learn of that. And she expressed the society's concern that if the link was significant it should be noted in some way and it would certainly be sad to see the Fen disappear under a building site.

The affluence of the members was stressed in the letter, in which Mme Clemency made it clear that funding would be no object to anything they decided to do by way of conserving Chateaubriand's memory permanently in Bungay.

And - which gave Danny particular optimism - she had agreed to travel to Bungay at the end of August with the society's chairman, Compte Phillippe de Bouchier, to visit the Fen and talk to campaigners, and the developers if possible, about its historic link and its future. This could be the answer to his prayers.

The Save Our Fen group was enthusiastic about the visit, and it certainly had plenty of publicity possibilities - it brought an international element to the campaign, and plans were made to give the party a civic welcome by the Town Reeve and the Mayor, and a tour of the whole town, with lunch at the Fisher Theatre café bar before going to the Fen for a walk around the Hards and Lows, and beside the river. A trip by rowing boat on the river was also organised so the French visitors could enjoy at first hand the amenities the Fen offered as it was.

Danny's hope, perhaps naively, was that the Chateaubriand link, with its high standing in the history of Europe as a whole and England, could be powerful enough to bring pressure to bear on George Bell and Pilgrim to abandon their plan to desecrate the Fen and

Iris Glade - perhaps in return for some favours they could do on building sites in France where there was not the same environmental pressure, and where the possibilities could be just as lucrative.

But the visit did not go as the SOF action group or Danny had hoped.

"C'est tres beau - it is very beautiful," said Mme Clemency as she and Compte Phillippe surveyed Outney common in the August sunshine with Danny, other members of the campaign group, Fenny, and George Bell, who had, again reluctantly, agreed to be there.

"To think that Chateaubriand was familiar with this land and walked here regularly with Charlotte is exciting for us. It is right that his presence here should be preserved and marked in a permanent way."

The French accent was strong, but her English was near perfect.

"That is correct," said Compte Phillippe. "In France his romance with Charlotte is seen as a significant part of his life, and we have visited Bungay before, to see the house where he stayed and the other towns he stayed at, but this area was not known to us as one he knew well. We would like to be involved in marking that here in some way - creating the Chateaubriand Park or something like that."

Danny was buoyed by that remark.

"That is a something we would very much support - any scheme that would preserve the Fen as it is rather than see it disappear as a building site," he said. "That is going to happen in just a couple of weeks unless we can persuade Mr Bell here to drop his scheme. But if we could do that, there would be the question of buying the site back from his company, and we have no funds."

"There would be funds available in France, I can assure you," said Compte Phillippe, whose demeanour and the way he presented himself suggested he was from a wealthy family. "The members of our group could raise almost any amount of money if we thought that would be the right thing to do. But first..."

He was interrupted by George Bell.

"May I say, Madame and Monsieur, that the design of our scheme includes a central park. We would be more than happy to name that the Compte Francois de Chateaubriand Memorial Park, and ourselves provide a suitable plaque to note that. Or indeed we could provide a statue of Chateaubriand and Charlotte as a central focus for the park, together with an information board detailing his time in Bungay and his love of Charlotte."

"That sounds an ideal proposal, Monsieur," said Madame Clemency. "I'm sure our members would be delighted with that and we could discuss the commissioning of such a statue and who should pay for it. Our members would certainly contribute. For us it could become a memorial to his time in England as a whole - he was Ambassador to the court of King George IV, but we know of no other memorial anywhere to his important links with your country."

Danny's heart sank as quickly as it had been lifted a couple of minutes earlier. George Bell certainly thought quickly to come up with his proposal and clearly the French visitors saw it is a perfect compromise.

"But it was the whole of this Fen that Chateaubriand knew, not just a part of it - surely it would be more appropriate, more faithful to his memory if the whole area was preserved as it is. And that would also retain it as an amenity for the people of our town," he said, in a bid to retrieve the situation. There were loud murmurs of support from the other members of the campaign group.

"Chateaubriand was a diplomat - he above anyone would see this as a solution that should suit everyone, and retain the friendship between our two countries," said Mme Clemency, with a chilling finality in her tone.

"Thank you, Monsieur Bell. Our organisation is delighted with your offer and we will confirm it in writing as soon as we return to France. There will be plenty of time to compile the details of the scheme before the time comes when the development is ready to have a statue installed."

George Bell shook the hands of the two visitors warmly to intimate his agreement with their view.

"Now," Mme Clemency added in a business like way, "We would very much like to take a walk around the Fen to feel the footsteps that Chateaubriand trod more than two centuries ago."

Danny and the campaigners watched them go, escorted by the courteous Fenny. George Bell declined the invitation and hurried off.

What had momentarily seemed hopeful, had gone sadly wrong. What avenue was there now left for the campaigners to explore in their bid to save Outney from the bulldozers?

CHAPTER TWENTY

SEPTEMBER 1st dawned clear and sunny, heralding autumn with a warmth and mellowness over a Suffolk countryside that had been dry now for three weeks. The scents of the hedgerows and verges reflected the early bronze and gold that autumn would eventually bring fully as it bridged the season to winter.

It was the season so eloquently described by one poet as "the season of mists and mellow fruitfulness," and the writer must have had somewhere like the Fen in mind as he wrote those words. The blackberries were ripe for picking, acorns were beginning to fall from the oak trees, some of them, in time, destined to become tiny shoots that would become mighty oaks one day, prickly horse chestnuts just on the other side of the river would soon be splitting to spill their shiny brown fruit, and hazelnuts to be found here and there were ripening.

As Danny and Megan approached the Fen from Broad Street that morning he was confronted by security fencing, decorated with red and white "Keep Out - building site" signs, with mechanical diggers and bulldozers lined up inside ready to go to work in earnest later that day on the delayed Iris Glade project.

But they were determined to take one last, emotional walk on the Fen's green and golden acres, to trace the paths once more, stroll through the high grass through the Iris Glade curtain, to enjoy the mingling scents and sounds in the land of the barn owl, heron, otter and kingfisher which would no more be seen there again, chased from their habitats by commercial muscle, adding to the worrying statistics of species decline which would fuel more articles of concern in newspapers and magazines. People would sympathise with them, but few would try to do anything to change the trend.

They managed to push through a gap in the fencing on to the Fen and make their way along their familiar route. Was the autumn mantle now being assumed by the Fen its most beautiful? Favourite season? An age-old question that some had firm views on, but one on which Danny always wavered - there was so much to commend each season of the year on the Fen. It was simply a matter of enjoying each one in its turn.

Now, this autumn would be the last the Fen would see, the final opportunity to enjoy the landscape until now largely untouched by human hand. Already the cattle had gone, the farmers having found other pasture for them, the golf course had been abandoned some months ago in anticipation of work on the scheme starting.

But the blackberries still flourished, the bright purple splashed of willowherb were everywhere, the skylark still soared to the heights under the blue sky, and Danny spotted a heron over on the Lows gently flapping to a smooth landing beside one of the dykes.

As he passed through Iris Glade towards the river, he looked up to glimpse again the sky through the still green foliage of the birch trees - that beautiful sight linking land and heaven, one which had symbolised contentment for him since his childhood days.

The spot where Jenny had died was still identified by many flowers placed there by many friends and supporters. Most had crumbled and rotted over the weeks, but he noticed that there were a dozen or so fresh bunches laid there, probably the previous day. The day after she had died he had lain some himself, but since then had preferred to keep fresh flowers beside her picture he kept on the chest of drawers in his bedroom.

That September morning the flowers all had messages on. He squatted down to look at some of them:

"Remembering Jenny, a true fighter," said one, anonymously; and another; "Jenny, no buildings here will overshadow your memory." And a third: "Peace to you Jenny, in this beautiful place."

There were others in a similar vein. Danny was about to stand up again when another, almost concealed message, caught his eye because of the name on it. In a small child's hesitant and uneven writing it read:

"Miss Rogers, if I could stop them digging up the Fen I would. We all love you. Chloe and Class 2."

It brought a lump to Danny's throat as he stood up and looked around the Outney panorama again.

"Dear Chloe, that goes for all of us," he said to himself, as Megan eagerly moved on ahead of him to the distant end of the Fen, hazy in the early morning sun.

"Even at this last minute, what can we do? We've tried so many things, said the right things, made the right pleas, contacted the right people - said the right prayers, haven't we?

"Yet here we are, and nothing has changed. This sanctuary of ours is about to disappear. The time is near. Within two hours the machinery will be moving in."

Megan looked up at him eagerly, and then ran off into the gorse and blackberry bushes, now heavy with their final fruiting, but remaining unpicked and soon to be devoured only by the earthmovers.

They moved on through the Fen that autumn day, yet seasons do not take on their mantle exactly on the due day, and so it was at this time - it was still summer there, despite September arriving, and it was going to be a warm day. Yet perhaps there was a hint in the common aromas of the beginning of autumn, as the fruits offered themselves for harvest, the sap began to settle in the tall grasses and swifts and sand martins began to prepare for their southerly migration.

Through the curtain of trees into Iris Glade he moved with Megan. How she would miss this scene - where would her next walk be?

As they moved into the glade and Danny looked towards the bridge, he saw a figure there, leaning on the rail, head down, looking into the dyke below. As he got nearer, he realised it was George Bell. What on earth was he doing there, at that time, in the morning, with work about to start on his major project?

The big man straightened as he saw Megan and Danny approach the bridge.

"Morning Mr Tegerdine. I suppose I should have known you would have been here today."

His voice sounded weary and pre-occupied.

"I'm sure you've realised already that this is my second home."

Having said it, he realised there was something slightly Freudian about the remark.

"I think you have got your feelings about this place over fairly clearly to everyone. And I agree - it is a beautiful place."

"So at what time do the bulldozers move in to change that forever?" said Danny, with ironic coldness.

George Bell looked at him with an expression that seemed vacant, troubled. Then he lent on the bridge rail again and looked down into the water. He drew a deep breath, and breathed out slowly.

"Mr Tegerdine, let me tell you something. I started out in life with nothing - my parents were poor as church mice, I had no real childhood as you knew it here, in surroundings like this" - he made a wide gesture with one arm - "with peace, and security, the chance of good qualification at a good school.

"I had nothing, and learnt nothing. The only thing I learnt was that anything you got you had to work for, even just to get money for a sandwich or a cup of coffee. So I decided at a young age that I was going to work - for myself, to achieve something my parents would be proud of."

He paused, before looking up from his leaning position, towards Danny, and continuing:

"They did not live to see that happen - they died in poverty. That made me all the more determined to make something of my life, to make my fortune by sheer hard work, and provide a secure future for my family. I almost built Pilgrim's with my own bare hands.

"But...I don't know..." he looked down again, wearily. "...I suppose I forgot about my roots for a while - not just my parents, but the people in our part of London, the community. I was too busy making money and, yes, in some ways it was at the expense of other people, other companies - other people's jobs perhaps. But that is the world of business - it is hard, and can be cruel, and sometimes there are no rules."

Danny listened intently as George Bell went through what was clearly some sort of soul searching, evaluating his life and what it stood for. He had done so himself after hearing the evidence of the now exposed Yvonne Delgardo. Maybe it was she he had partly in mind when he spoke about there being no rules.

The big man was silent for a while. Then he went on:

"When you head a business as big as mine, you live two lives - your business and your family. Only your family seems to have a smaller and smaller part in it the bigger the business gets. That's what has happened to me, Mr Tegerdine, and you know, that suddenly came home to me the other day.

"I've got a big family - six children, and I've almost lost count of the number of grandchildren. They are all good, all lovely kids. But when you are wrapped up in a business as big as mine you hardly see them, you know. Have you got children Mr Tegerdine?"

"No, no I haven't, yet anyway. My children are those in my school."

"Yes, yes of course. Not quite the same though. No, I don't see them nearly as much as I would like. They are all secure financially, I've seen to that, mind. And I always tell them that if there is anything they want, they can have it - just let me know. Yes -" an unexpected smile broke out on his face as he turned it towards Danny again. "- yes, that is something I can do for them, and it makes me feel good."

Then the smile was gone and the haunted look returned to the big man's face.

" But I can tell you this, Mr Tegerdine, There is one I would love to have the chance to do anything for, and I can't, I can't."

Danny's demeanour was changing from one of indifference to one of curious interest. He could see George Bell was beginning to struggle for words.

"Do you want to tell me why?" he said gently.

Again there was silence. The big man straightened up again, moved to the other side of the narrow bridge, looked around at the Vineyard Hills and then turned to look out over the Fen towards Bungay. He looked at Danny, and held his eyes for some seconds, before leaning on the rail again.

"I actually had seven children - four sons and three daughters," he began, slowly. "The youngest of them all was Ellie. Well, I'm an ugly brute, but she was the prettiest little girl you ever saw - brown eyes, dark hair, smiling mouth and eyes, a cheeky grin. A bit of a tomboy. Parents don't have favourites, but they do, in a quiet unspoken sort of way. And Ellie was mine. I told them all that if there was anything, anything they wanted to ask for, I would give it to them, or find it for them, or do it for them, whatever it was, and I have tried to be true to that.

"I've been lucky. I've spent most of my life working to make money, and in today's terms I've made many millions. Yet my children rarely asked for expensive material things. Wealth didn't seem to be a priority for them as it has been for me."

He paused, and again drew a deep breath.

"You said you didn't have the chance to do anything for Ellie," Danny ventured. "Why - why was that?"

George Bell put his head in his hands.

"My Ellie died, when she was only seven," he said, almost inaudible with emotion. "She drowned in one of the ponds on Wimbledon Common. I…I was nearby, but I wasn't…I wasn't aware of what was happening, till it was too late. Her brothers and sisters were screaming, but I thought they were playing. I stood about 100 yards away talking to a chap about another property deal."

He let out an audible moan.

"That was 30 years ago and still it haunts me, still it tears into me, still it breaks me up, y'know."

"It must be very hard for you, losing someone like that, at that age. Especially a daughter."

Danny was genuinely sympathetic now, not quite sure what to say. But he added:

"I guess losing Jenny in such awful circumstances I have some idea…" his words trailed off.

"Oh, for most of the time you come to terms with it, and control it. Time heals to an extent. And then suddenly without warning something or someone will bring it all back to the front of your mind."

Again a pause, before George Bell added, in a breaking voice: "That's what happened a couple of weeks ago and it's been in my mind ever since."

The big corporate chairman had suddenly become human, vulnerable, his emotions close to the surface, and Danny began to see him in a different light. Again he said gently:

"Do you want to tell me about that."

Clearly he was now struggling for composure, his face still fixed firmly on the water below the bridge on which he leaned ever more heavily.

"You were there, Mr Tegerdine, it was just over there, at the top of the rise, at your open air service. It was that little girl, Chloe. It made me feel…I don't know, I can't describe it…You would find words for it. It was spooky."

He seemed to be making a supreme effort, but hesitating as if he was not sure whether to continue, there, in the quietness of the morning, beside the silent river, as Danny and Megan stood waiting expectantly.

Eventually he did.

"It was Ellie there, talking to me, pleading with me. It was her, for a few seconds she even spoke in the way Ellie did sometimes - earnestly, as if life depended on what she said. It took my breath away I can tell you."

Now it was Danny turn to feel a sensation run through his whole body as the big man spoke those words. Suddenly, he felt a bond with him.

"George, that is quite uncanny. It is unbelievable. When Chloe spoke to me about the Common, in her childlike way, I saw a young Jenny standing there in front of me."

George Bell straightened up. The two men looked at each other on that narrow, rustic bridge, not hearing the splash of an otter nearby, or the skylark's latest symphony.

They were dwelling on a compelling message, the same message, from lost loved ones - Jenny and Ellie, both speaking their plea through the voice of innocence. Through Chloe.

Not a muscle moved on the big man's face. But a single tear fell from the corner of each eye.

"It came from out of this world, but I cannot reject that plea. I'm abandoning the Iris Glade project. It's all off. It's what Ellie would have wanted."

"It's what Jenny would have wanted, too. But…are you sure?"

"Yes, I'm sure. I instructed the company secretary and the site manager before I came down here this morning. This Fen remains as it is."

The two men held eye contact for several moments, there on the bridge over the dyke, by the meadows and river at the foot of the hills by Bungay, in rural Suffolk. Two opposites in personality and outlook, brought to a common view by the simply-stated words of a little girl free of the impediments of corporate finance, or balance sheets, or commerce, or planning applications - or even knowledge of what the Fen stood for environmentally.

"You know," said George Bell, slowly. "I somehow

feel relieved - a weight off my shoulders, content. Ellie was not like the others, she never asked me for anything material. But maybe this is the gift she would have asked me for, if she had been able to."

Eventually, Danny stretched out his hand to the big man who he suddenly had some admiration for. George Bell took it, and held it in firm, silent affirmation.

And suddenly Danny was aware of the soaring skylark, high above, composing a triumphant concerto.

The two men walked back together, a relieved Megan ahead of them, along the path through the tall grass, towards the curtain of trees through which they would go as they left Iris Glade, its natural future secure. The sounds of the common were there - the breeze in the grass and trees, the grasshoppers, the linnets, the occasional mooing from the cattle on the Lows. The sun was climbing in the sky warmly to the south-east, and St Mary's Church and the roofs of the town were visible ahead. It was as it had ever been.

There was no noise of earthmovers and site equipment, as Danny had expected when he went there that morning, no scarring of the common ground. And he uttered a silent prayer of thanks.

The two men moved through the curtain of silver birches and oaks and high-growing brambles. As they came out the other side they saw four men approaching them, one of them in police uniform. Danny's immediate thought was that they were checking that there was no trouble on what should have been the day work started - no doubt there would be more at the entrance to the common to convey the news that the scheme had been shelved..

But he was badly mistaken. The group came up to them purposefully, stopped, and one of the suited men said:

"Mr Bell - Mr George Bell?"

"Yes, that's me."

"Mr Bell, we're here to arrest you on suspicion of conspiracy to murder Robin Anderson at Wattisfield on July 16th, 2005..."

The startled Danny looked at the big man, who visibly tensed and paled.

"What…?" he uttered.

"We have sufficient evidence to take you for questioning. You don't have to say anything, but anything you do say may be used in evidence at any trial."

George Bell looked despairingly at Danny for a moment, his eyes wide, a half indignant, half frightened look on his face. He trembled. But he said nothing more, and allowed himself to be led away, back to the town.

Danny hesitated, undecided whether he should walk back with them, but in the end he walked back on his own, by another path. He was completely stunned by the events of the morning, and wanted to collate them in is head.

Above all he wanted to convince himself that the Fen, after all, was to be left as it had always been…

CHAPTER TWENTY-ONE

IF HE needed convincing, that came that evening on television and radio, and the following day in the newspapers. It was sensational news, totally unexpected, and the media had a field day, both on George Bell's sudden change of heart and his arrest on the conspiracy to murder charge. There were interviews, background stories, a review of what had happened over the near two-year period since the plan was first revealed, and the tragedies that had occurred. The Gazette devoted six pages to it, with pictures of all the main protagonists, and a separate feature on the Fen, concentrating on its unchanging beauty, with a portfolio of stunning pictures to illustrate it.

And there was a strap heading across those two pages: *The tiny voice giant tycoon George could not resist.*

They had managed to get hold of a picture of Ellie, and also one of Chloe, and Danny was amazed at the uncanny similarities between the two. The tragic story of Ellie's death was recounted. It had happened 15 years ago, and at that time, prophetically, one national newspaper had quoted George Bell as saying; "Clearly we are all heart-broken. If only a miracle could happen and she could be brought back, I would grant her any wish under the sun."

Jubilant scenes in Bungay town centre of celebrating Save Our Fen campaigners, with their elated comments, were also given considerable prominence, along with more subdued comments from town council chairman Andrew Neill-Davids and chamber of trade president Sally Webster.

But the key part of the coverage surrounded a statement from George Bell's solicitor:

"For obvious legal reasons I cannot comment on Mr Bell's arrest and the nature of the charge against him.

Suffice it to say that we will study very carefully the evidence from which the charge resulted.

"As far as the decision to call off the Iris Glade project is concerned it was not, as has been reported, a sudden decision. A number of factors and a number of problems with the design of the scheme for such a low-lying site had been brought to our attention at a late hour, and while they were certainly not insurmountable in modern technical terms, the solutions were particularly costly. That had implications for our profit margins and Mr Bell had been studying that in more detail.

"At the same time, he is his own man, and he was not immune from the considerable local opposition to Iris Glade and the strong emotional links many people in the town have with the area. He, with the confirmation of the board, has therefore decided to withdraw the scheme. We apologise that the decision has come at a late hour, but it is a firm and final one.

"The Fen will remain in the ownership of Pilgrim's and George Bell. The company will be responsible for its future management, and we are already taking steps to impose a convenant on it which will prevent any building development by Pilgrim or any other company taking place on it in the future.

"We also apologise to our contractors and sub-contractors who have planned this into their work schedules for some considerable time ahead, but alternative work will be found for them on other sites within the region where on-going developments are not so sensitive."

Danny read each report keenly, still scarcely able to take in the dramatic and sudden turn of events. Yet his elation that the Fen's future seemed to be secure was tempered by two thoughts:

One was that he had made a sudden decision to withdraw his opposition to the scheme not so many months ago, only for later events to lead him to change his mind. Was that still a possibility with George Bell? He knew more about his personality now, but still not a great deal. If he was a vindictive man could the charges against him lead him to revert to his original plan after mulling things over for a few days?

The other thought was that if he remained true to his word, the lives of Robin Anderson and Jenny had been needlessly sacrificed.

Those were among his comments to Bill Burdock when the editor finally managed to get hold of him for his comments on the story.

That evening, with Megan, he went into the subdued light and sanctity of Holy Trinity Church, and knelt at the altar to offer prayers of thanks. The light from the evening sun shone through the Sunday School window, illuminating the circled auras around the heads of the child figures. The determination and faith that had achieved that simple window came to him again.

And he noticed another thing. The butterfly was nowhere to be seen. Had its unwavering battle for the freedom of the outdoors finally been won?

When Danny later made for the Fen, it was almost with trepidation. There was still a flickering sense of doubt that all was well after all, that something else could happen to snatch the good news away. But once there among its familiar comforts and evening shadows, the doubts melted way. Now he was sure that it would endure, perhaps for another 1000 years.

And he knew the spirit of Jenny would be there always - the spirit of the Fen, to talk to whenever he and Megan went there.

As the sun sunk behind the Vineyard Hills and he wandered among the shadows and along Waveney's banks, his mind went back over the whole saga, the whole battle to keep Outney Fen as it was, as it was always meant to be, and the gamut of contrasting emotions it had brought out among many people on both sides. There had been ugly feelings, almost evil in some cases, a lot of anger, a lot of determination, many tears of emotion and tragedy, and certainly there had been the emotion of greed.

But there had been feelings of love and compassion, too, and of courage to do what people genuinely thought was right. In the end, George Bell had shown huge courage in his decision to end the scheme in the face of what must have been angry opposition from the rest of the board of Pilgrim's.

Yes, Danny, thought, there had been changing emotions in many people, and perhaps none more so than in George Bell - the rightful feelings to provide well for his family, the harshness that running a big business calls for, the greed that brought out the evil in him to stop at nothing to win planning permission, and finally the love and compassion that led him to a momentous change of heart through the pleas of a small girl.

"Out of the mouths of babes..."

Maybe his Gran had been wide of the mark after all on her theory of emotions. They are all there, latently, in everyone, and while personalities are formed by a predominant emotion, circumstances can bring different ones, good or bad, to the surface at any time, in any but the strongest of characters - those with the greatest spiritual strength. From embryo, the whole range remains with everyone till death.

"Peter?"

The gentle but sure voice startled Danny abruptly from his musing, and sent a shiver down his spine as he immediately turned towards the direction from which it had come. He was back in the curtain of trees leading into Iris Glade, and the light had almost completely gone. But he made out the shape of the old, cloaked, white-bearded figure, with a staff in his hand, he had seen before.

"Peter? Yes, you are Peter."

He held Danny's startled gaze for a moment, and a smile of kindness and recognition lightened his pale face and sunken eyes. Then he was gone again, melting into the shadows as suddenly as he had appeared.

"Wait..."

Danny took a step forward, but there were only the silhouettes of the trees and brambles to be seen through the darkness, and beyond, in the night sky, a new crescent moon. And he stopped, and turned again towards the towered town.

"Peter - the rock on which I will build my church." And the ghostly figure, who in a previous meeting had said, "No, you're not Peter," now seemed to have changed his mind, thought Danny, still shaky from the uncanny, ghostly encounter.

Pontius Pilate, Judas, Peter - three men he saw as key figures of the New Testament. And suddenly he realised he had been called all of them over the past two years as he battled with his own views and feelings in the campaign to protect Bungay's best loved natural asset:

The weak-willed traitor; the man without the courage of his convictions, protecting his own interests ahead of doing what he knew was right; and the man of inner spiritual strength. He had even had murder in mind at one moment.

All these had come to him at different times. And he was all of them - and none. Simply one human being with all the human frailties, hopes and dreams which had to compromise with reality.

He found himself on the bridge, in the deep twilight, once more, Megan dutifully beside him. He looked around on either side, at the meadows, the trees, the Vineyard Hills, the glow of the lights from Vineyard House, to the pin-prick stars and the waxing moon. And he saw Jenny too, in his mind.

"My dear, dear Jenny...I know you are there, somewhere, in this heaven that is Bungay Fen - you will always be here, and I will come, and stand on our bridge, and muse with you often, as if you were here as we used to be. Yes, Jen, yes - because thanks to you the battle was won. There will be no building here....Iris Glade will remain, this green and pleasant sanctuary will remain, and the owls and otters and herons and swans and cygnets and cuckoos and kingfishers, they and many others will have their home here.

"And people will come here still, to play and roam and swim and find peace and contentment, and walk with God. And your spirit will be here always, my darling - the spirit of the Fen which never dies, and which never lost faith when others doubted. And I will keep your sweet smile in my heart always..."

Danny bowed his head. All around him was still, silent, the familiar silhouettes stood waiting.

And from the still air the silence was broken by a breeze which gently ruffled the leaves and the grasses close by, and caressed his face for a held instant. Then it was gone, and complete quietness returned.

Danny absorbed the moment, and then stood straight and said:

"Come on Megan - let's go home."

George Bell was ultimately charged with the lesser indictment of conspiracy to cause harm to Robin Anderson. It transpired that the driver of the van which knocked him off the road, causing his death, had been contracted by George Bell, in the words he used in court, "to try to ensure that he did not get to the planning meeting in Lowestoft that evening. I admit that. But I utterly and completely deny any suggestion that I wanted physical harm done to Mr Anderson, and I deeply regret his death."

The van driver, Frank Dalliston, had apparently contacted the police after failing to receive payment for his "work" from George Bell or Pilgrim's - he said he had been told he would receive £5000. He also confirmed that he had simply been asked to prevent Mr Anderson getting to the meeting, and had not meant to harm him.

Had he not spoken of the deal Robin Anderson's death might have remained, officially, as an accident - the verdict at his inquest.

Both Bell and Dalliston also admitted to charges of conspiracy to pervert the course of justice, and Dalliston was also charged with causing death by dangerous driving. Bell was sentenced to three years in jail and Dalliston two years. They both got off lightly, Danny felt.

Despite their meeting on the Fen, and seeing the big man in a different, human light, he could find little sympathy for him. The planning permission for the Iris Glade project remained on the books, with the Government's Planning Inspectorate deciding that "notwithstanding the offences that have come to light surrounding evidence given both to the district council and to the planning inquiry, the decision to allow the project remains sound on planning grounds alone."

But the Gazette, and indeed the national press and television, conjectured that the permission for the project would remain tainted by the happenings surrounding it for many years - certainly beyond the time by which the planning permission would lapse, and that it would probably never be resurrected. A long and dramatic saga that had seen two people die in what they now called The battle of Iris Glade would be enough to ensure that.

It was a victory for the town and the people of Bungay - hard won and at a heavy price. Perhaps too great a price.

Outney Fen remained in the ownership of George Bell and Pilgrim's. There was no move to sell it back to the Fen Wardens (who would probably have declined anyway). It remained as it had always been - pastureland and heathland, a place for people to walk and play and swim and enjoy nature and have their thoughts inspired by the surroundings.

There was to be no building on those acres, though the golf course was eventually re-established and the club flourished again.

Except one structure was sited there. Six months after George Bell was released from prison, a statue was erected in Iris Glade. It was unheralded, and without publicity. For many who walked there, it would seem to have suddenly appeared, there, beside the river, beside the bridge.

It was of a young woman, and a young girl, the older looking down at the river, the younger looking up towards the sky, as if seeing, between them, eternally, the splash of the otter, the electric blue of the darting kingfisher, the serene swans and cygnets, the water lilies and the flag irises along the river, and the slow journey of the heron, the soaring skylark, the searching, systematic flight of the barn owl, and beyond, the trees and the outline of Bungay. Steadfast and unchanging, surrounded for ever by the peace, the beauty and the sense of contentment with which the Fen enfolds all its visitors.

The inscription on the statue read, simply:

Jenny and Ellie.

Printed in the United Kingdom
by Lightning Source UK Ltd.
128372UK00001B/148-345/P

9 781846 859496